We Do What We Do
in the Dark

We Do What We Do
in the Dark

Michelle Hart

RIVERHEAD BOOKS | NEW YORK | 2022

RIVERHEAD BOOKS
An imprint of Penguin Random House LLC
penguinrandomhouse.com

Library of Congress Cataloging-in-Publication Data
Names: Hart, Michelle, author.
Title: We do what we do in the dark / Michelle Hart.
Description: New York : Riverhead Books, 2022. |
Identifiers: LCCN 2021027954 (print) | LCCN 2021027955 (ebook) |
ISBN 9780593329672 (hardcover) | ISBN 9780593329696 (ebook)
Subjects: LCGFT: Fiction.
Classification: LCC PS3608.A78655 W4 2022 (print) |
LCC PS3608.A78655 (ebook) | DDC 813/.6—dc23
LC record available at https://lccn.loc.gov/2021027954
LC ebook record available at https://lccn.loc.gov/2021027955

International edition ISBN: 9780593541500

Printed in the United States of America
1   3   5   7   9   10   8   6   4   2

Book design by Amanda Dewey

We Do What We Do
in the Dark

The Woman

When Mallory was in college, she had an affair with a woman twice her age. When the woman was seventeen, she herself had had an affair with a man in his forties. Mallory admired the woman so much that, for many years, any similarity between them flattered her.

Mallory had run on the treadmill behind the woman at the university's gym for weeks before they actually met. It was September of her freshman year. Mallory, whose mother had died months before, had become haunted by the prospect of poor health. Also, she was a first-year student and worried about letting something free, like a gym membership, go to waste.

The school's main gym was in the midst of renovations; a crude, makeshift workout area now occupied one half of the intramural basketball court. This was separated from the other half by a large mesh curtain. The treadmills and weight-lifting equipment were laid atop a foundation of cardboard flooring so as not to scuff the hardwood underneath. It was a squalid, airless space, almost like a hospital, with nowhere pleasing to look.

Mallory felt drawn to the woman the first time she saw her.

The woman had walked into the gym wearing a loose-fitting tank top so slack it billowed as she moved. She carried an alluring sadness about her, with dark pouches under her eyes that seemed to hold a lot of weariness and wisdom. The woman's facial expression dramatized the solitude Mallory herself felt inside. The woman wore it well, and as her shirt lifted from her body, Mallory saw the woman's melancholy as an invitation, a shared space for the two of them.

Tied to the woman's wrist was a small, folded towel, and when the woman stepped onto the treadmill, she unwound it, draping it over the machine's control panel so the buttons and the time were hidden. She worked out on her own internal clock, without headphones, intensely focused and free of distraction. As the woman ran, Mallory looked from her shoulder blades, which Mallory's mother had called "wings," to her ass. The woman had a body that was taut and muscular. It was the kind of body that seemed like it would never be stricken by illness.

The woman, Mallory learned, went to the gym at the same time every other day. She ran three miles in twenty-four minutes. In that period, Mallory could hardly run two, but she found watching the woman made the time tick heedlessly.

Seeing how fit the woman was, Mallory began to eat healthier. Instead of a bagel at breakfast, she had a banana or some yogurt. Instead of a sandwich for lunch, she ate a salad. By the end of her first month away at school, she'd burned off most of the baby fat she still carried with her. After eighteen years of avoiding her reflection, or else being preoccupied by its abject homeliness, she now stood for long, surreptitious spells in front of the mirror in the communal bathroom with her shirt hiked up.

The university Mallory attended was on Long Island. The campus, a forty-five-minute train ride from Manhattan, lay between two towns——one said to be seedy, the other considered posh. The bad part had the bars, where some of the students went on weekends, since they were within walking distance; the good, which was harder to access without a car, had the manicured lawns of the professors' homes.

The college was mostly a commuter school, and on nights and weekends it was as if two-thirds of the students simply vanished, like the Rapture. Lacking both a car and an interest in bars, Mallory felt at once claustrophobic and isolated, a feeling with which she had been familiar for most of her life. She'd hoped college would be different. Her body vibrated with potential energy. But walking to and from her classes, she saw the sprawling campus as indifferent to her. She had the perpetual feeling of sneezing without being blessed.

Other than her roommate, whose name was Joy, Mallory hadn't made any new friends. Together their dorm room was a pair of Greek theater masks: Joy on one side, Mallory on the other. Joy had come to the college to study drama. She had the looks and the disposition for acting. Many things she did seemed dramatic: When she spoke or ate, she obscured her mouth with the back of her hand. When she read, she sometimes shut the book and bit into its jacket. When she watched shows on her laptop, she blinked rapidly and forcefully as if she was wincing, or willing something into happening like Barbara Eden in *I Dream of Jeannie.*

Joy had spent much of their first few weeks at school preparing to audition for the school's play. She rehearsed monologues from Shakespeare and her favorite films. Some of these she performed for Mallory. But she didn't get a part. This devastated her, and for days after her audition, she became withdrawn. During this time, Mallory felt embarrassed on both of their behalf; the humiliation of a ruined dream was too acute, and Mallory felt incapable of consoling her. Time passed, however, and Joy declared that the following semester she would study prelaw. The courtroom was a different kind of theater, she said, and one that paid much better. Her tossing aside an old life so easily brought Mallory comfort; a new one might be waiting for her, too.

❦

On a Tuesday night at the end of September, Mallory spoke to the woman for the first time. The university was hosting a visiting writer. Because she was studying literature, and because the writer's book jacket had "bestseller" emblazoned on it, Mallory thought she ought to go.

There were cookies by the entrance of the small auditorium where the visiting writer read. Mallory put one on a clear plastic dish and filled a paper cup with black coffee. She sat by herself in the last row. She broke the cookie in half and broke the half in half before sliding it daintily between her lips. As she chewed, she held a hand in front of her mouth, ladylike, the way Joy ate.

She saw the woman sitting in the second row. The woman's head was bowed as if reading a book in her lap. Her blond hair had been pulled loose from the ponytail she wore at the gym and hung down to her shoulders. Mallory had run on the treadmill behind her so often by then that she could make out the woman from many rows back.

An older man, the chair of the English department, called the small crowd to attention. This prompted the woman to look back and survey the room. In doing so, she found Mallory. Mallory looked away, but when she looked back, the woman's eyes were still on her. The woman's hair was parted down the middle such that both sides appeared as the arches of a lowercase "m." Mallory fingered the tips of her own hair, the way her mother had worried the ends of her wig when meeting someone new.

Before she began reading, the visiting writer, who possessed a free-spirited frumpiness that made her appear as a soothsayer, told a story about riding the subway in New York City weeks earlier. On the train, she said, she had sat across from a man reading a newspaper. He was bald and had bags under his eyes. The newspaper was from September 12, 2001. The writer had done a double take to make sure she wasn't hallucinating. The man was reading over the news in a distressed daze, as if the disaster had happened the previous day, though it was now seven years later. Watching him made the writer's heart sink. She wondered whether the man was a writer himself, a trauma survivor, or a time traveler. Getting off at her stop, she thought, *Those might all be the same thing.*

Uneasy, fragmented laughter scattered throughout the auditorium. No one knew whether the anecdote was meant as a joke.

The writer then read from her most recent novel, which was set sometime in the sixties, when the author herself had been a young girl. It involved sexual abuse. As the writer read, Mallory drifted off. She fantasized about her own future fame, or at least what it might feel like to be seen and revered for her experiences and ideas. She had plenty of the latter but few of the former.

After the reading was over, and after a short Q&A, the woman slid herself from her seat and made for the auditorium's exit. Mallory, feeling bold, fled after her.

She followed the woman into the bathroom. The woman went into one of the stalls, and Mallory stood in front of the wide mirror above the sinks, rocking back and forth on her heels. The woman's urination echoed in the empty restroom. Thinking the woman might be embarrassed by the sound, Mallory turned on the sink, which was automatic; this meant she had to constantly wave her hand underneath the tap to keep the water on. She pumped soap into her hand and washed it off. All possible vestiges of the soap had been scrubbed away when, finally, the woman emerged from the stall.

Watching the woman move in the mirror, Mallory pulled a paper towel from the ream. She pulled too many and offered the surplus to the woman.

"Thank you," the woman said, once she was done washing her hands. She spoke with a slight German lilt; what she said sounded more like "Sank you." "Where are the breath mints? The lotion?"

"Shoot," said Mallory. She patted herself down as if those things might appear.

They smiled at each other as if they'd been seated together on a once-turbulent plane now out of peril. Mallory was charmed and disarmed by the woman standing before her and could not think of anything else to say. Fantasies of meeting the woman had occurred so frequently she found the reality baffling. She opened her mouth to speak but then closed it, tasting the simple sweetness of the cookie she had eaten and the bitterness of the black coffee.

The woman balled up the paper towel and threw it out. She offered her name and asked Mallory's. Mallory did not like her name, but when the woman repeated it aloud—Mallory Green— it sounded somehow mellifluous, like it belonged in a storybook.

The woman pulled open the door. "Are you going back in?"

"I don't think I'm going to buy a book," said Mallory, "so it seems like I shouldn't."

"The book is not very good anyway," said the woman. "I was more interested in that man on the train." By themselves in the bathroom, in public but out of view, the woman's scorn gave Mallory a conspiratorial thrill.

They left the restroom and went their separate ways, peeling away from one another, Mallory felt, with reluctance.

S he found the woman's email address in the employee directory online. *It was nice meeting you the other night*, she wrote. The woman said back the same.

Over the next several days, they exchanged messages. Each email the woman returned felt like a gift. She asked which classes Mallory was taking, which books she was reading, which books she liked. Mallory could not remember any of them and asked her father to send a picture of her bookshelf back home. The photo he sent featured all her Goosebumps books and a Chronicles of Narnia boxed set.

Wanting to sound both fun and sophisticated, Mallory wrote to her about Nikolai Gogol and "The Nose," a story her high school English teacher had recommended to her the previous year, which she'd read over and over and even tried making into a comic. She told the woman she found the story both absurd and sort of sad; the body does what it wants.

According to the faculty directory, the woman was an adjunct and taught courses on children's literature. Through Google, Mallory learned the woman was also an author of picture books.

Mallory was sure she had misread this. She could not square the woman's weariness with the glee of stories for kids. But the books had won awards.

There was a video on YouTube of an interview the woman had given to PBS. As a young girl from Germany, she'd found America confounding and took comfort in the pleasingly static nature of picture books. She had started making her own when she was in grade school; she would sit in the corner of the classroom or under a tree on the playground and draw herself talking and playing with the other children, whom she was too afraid to speak to in real life. On paper, the woman said, everything could be safely contained.

With some of the money she'd saved up before college, Mallory ordered all the woman's books. When they arrived a few days later, she brought them to the quiet floor of the college library. The seclusion of the private study room and the faint musk of old books made reading the woman's work feel furtive, as if she was uncovering the woman's secret life. A soft, white light emanated from each page. There was something about the woman's books that beckoned Mallory into them. They said, *There is room enough for you here.*

With her own tracing paper, Mallory began copying the woman's art. The woman had lettered the books in her own handwriting; Mallory copied that, too.

❧

She went to see the woman at her office on campus. The office, which the woman occupied only twice a week, contained two desks facing away from one another against opposite walls. The woman kept the overhead light off; instead the room was lit solely by the sun soaking through a single window along the back wall. It felt like a monk's cell. The window overlooked a little courtyard with marble tables. Mallory could see and hear the other students outside. Visiting the woman, she felt her life was far away from theirs.

She went under the pretense of asking the woman what she should read. Doing this, she thought, would make her appear smart; also, if the woman gave her a book, she would have to bring it back, an excuse to see and talk to her again.

Mallory sat on a plastic chair beside the woman's desk. The woman asked her if she wanted to be a writer. Mallory looked at her hands in her lap. Her instinct was to say yes, but knowing the woman was an author, she wasn't sure she could say it.

"I used to draw," she said. Upon revealing this part of herself to the woman, her voice squeaked. "I mean, I still do. I used to think I was going to make comic books. But I'm worried I'm a better reader than I am a writer. Maybe I should have gone to art school."

Underneath the desk, the woman cracked each knuckle of her right hand. Before moving on to the left, she said, "Bad habit."

"I do that, too," Mallory said.

As if to keep her hand busy, the woman picked up a pen from her desk. She twiddled it between her index finger and thumb. "I had a boyfriend in graduate school whom people pleaded with to read and edit their work. He was very smart. We could talk for hours about stories, movies and books, and I learned a lot from him. He was always writing, but because we were dating,

I never wanted to read his work. If it was good, I would be jealous. If it was bad, I would no longer admire him."

"Was he any good?"

"He never published anything, so I have no idea. After school, he went to work as a paralegal at his father's law firm. I don't even know if he ever became an actual lawyer. That someone who meant a lot to me at one point did nothing meaningful with his life almost feels like a personal slight."

"See?" said Mallory, who felt both nervous and perversely inspired by the woman's high expectations for those close to her. "In high school, I read a lot and always spoke up in English class. I did things for the literary magazine—poems and short stories and cartoons. If I made something terrible now, people would say, 'That's it? That's what she amounted to?'"

"No one is thinking of you that way," said the woman. "No one is sitting around waiting for you to be good."

This felt damning, like a dismissal, yet it was also liberating. To be free of responsibility and expectation meant she could live her life the way she wanted to.

"You will be fine," the woman said after a while. "I can tell you're smart, much smarter than most of the people here."

Mallory beamed. "That means a lot coming from you."

"How did you end up here?"

"What do you mean?"

"What made you choose this school?"

Mallory told her that in kindergarten, the two-year-old brother of a boy in her class had accidentally strangled himself on a cord attached to venetian blinds. Because something dreadful happened to the boy and his family, Mallory had paid him more attention. In his extreme grief, he seemed more interesting to her. He had often worn a pullover sweatshirt with the name of the college printed on it. When she began looking at colleges, she became captivated by the idea of attending a school she coupled with doom.

A laugh ballooned from the woman's body, as if she wasn't expecting to find this funny. Mallory was accustomed to making people laugh; as a child, she'd been "the funny one." That she could make *this* woman laugh—a shrewd and elegant woman who was not so easily amused—made her feel as though she mattered.

She didn't tell the woman she had chosen the college while her mother was still alive. Her mother had also remembered the classmate's brother and the college sweatshirt. That her mother had recalled this morbid detail gladdened Mallory, and hearing the woman's laughter now in the face of such an awful thing consoled her.

∿

It was only after returning to her dorm room to do her homework that she realized she hadn't gotten any names of books to read from the woman. She looked through the syllabi of her current courses and thought it would not impress the woman to have read *Don Quixote* or *The Awakening*. She revisited the articles about the woman online, in the hopes of finding her recommendations, but the woman never talked about anyone else's books.

Two days later, she returned to the woman's office. The woman appeared pleasantly unsurprised to see her.

"Read Pushkin," the woman told her. "He's a lot of fun."

"Okay," Mallory said. "I will."

Since they still hadn't discussed it, she waffled over whether to disclose what she had learned about the woman online, that she was an author of picture books. But as a child, Mallory had been bad at hide-and-seek; the thrill of being found was almost physically painful, and she had to reveal herself right away. She said, "I kind of can't believe you make children's books."

The woman tilted her head to the side, genuinely curious why Mallory thought this. She looked as if the answer could hurt her. "Why?"

"You seem so sophisticated and serious."

"Because I'm German?"

"Maybe," Mallory said. "I like your accent. Is that a weird thing to say?"

"It depends on how much you like it."

They looked at each other. Mallory felt her cheeks and ears get hot. Her eyes fell back to her lap. But the woman gave Mallory's arm a playful poke. "It is not so easy. Many people I meet come up to me and say, 'I once told my child a story and he loved it; should I publish?' A lot of sophistication goes into making a book read so simply."

"I know," said Mallory. "I didn't mean it like that."

"Children are fickle. They get bored and confused and lose interest easily. They look for any reason to turn their attention elsewhere. The trick is to deny them this."

Mallory suspected that anyone wanting to befriend the woman, who saw it as her job to keep people—children—from looking away, had to do the same. Since it was so limited, what little attention the woman gave felt lavish.

The woman told Mallory to reread all the books she had loved as a child. The woman shook her head, however, when Mallory asked to borrow her copies, nudging Mallory to buy her own. Worried that she had already overextended the woman's patience, Mallory went to the school's bookstore and bought all the required texts for the woman's class.

In her dormitory bed, she flipped through books she'd read in what felt like a separate life from the one she was currently living: *Where the Wild Things Are*, *The Snowy Day*, *Harold and the Purple Crayon*. It was possible she'd never read these herself at all, that her mother, or an old teacher, had read them to her instead. She felt that, as a child, these stories had seemed to her to be about other children doing mischievous things, yet in the twin-sized bed of her college dorm, she had the feeling that she was reading about herself now. She saw the books anew: the way Maurice Sendak used the size of the artwork on the page to convey the character's emotional state, the way Crockett Johnson used white space to create possibility and suspense.

She tried to relay all this to the woman the next time she went to the woman's office, feeling breathless and raw. For a moment, she hoped the woman would invite her to take the class next semester; after all, she had already read the books. The woman only nodded, however, uninterested in any interpretation Mallory had to offer. The woman did not care whether the stories were read or what someone—what Mallory—thought of them. She had her own ideas about them, and anything else was noise. Confronted with the woman's indifference, Mallory felt as though she'd squeezed too much toothpaste from an already small tube.

Yet she was also enchanted by the idea of this woman who'd dedicated her life to teaching young people staying impervious to their contributions and whims. She admired the way the woman shucked off the world. This meant that if she found Mallory even a little worth her time, then Mallory's existence was truly worthwhile.

As she dithered over what to say next, two girls outside the woman's office window shrieked with laughter. Both Mallory and the woman turned to catch the source of the sound. The giggling girls walked on, unaware of being watched, and while Mallory's gaze remained trained on the window, the woman said, "I know what it's like." Mallory looked back at the woman, who continued: "To feel as though you have nothing to say to anyone your age."

Mallory shrugged.

"You don't need to feel left out. In fact, you will be better off if you are."

That separateness could be chosen, that it was the correct option, mollified Mallory.

In the second week of October, just after midterms, the woman invited Mallory to have dinner at her home. A few days before she went, Mallory bought a bottle of wine. She'd Googled "German wine" and purchased a bottle of Riesling from a nearby store known for selling alcohol to students.

The woman's house was a six-minute taxi ride from the college's campus. During the ride, Mallory passed storefronts and other houses done up with Halloween decorations—skeletons, pumpkins, cobwebs. She felt unexpectedly festive, as if she, too, was in costume. She was someone else, and what was happening was not real. She'd thought that things like this did not happen to girls like her, though maybe they did. A teacher in grade school had told her that if she went looking for trouble, trouble would find her, and Mallory wondered now whether this was the point at which she and trouble met in the middle. That she was at once responsible for what was happening and free from the responsibility of whatever would happen next so aroused her that she looked down at the wine bottle between her legs and started sliding an open fist up and down its neck.

When she arrived at the woman's house, she rang the bell and looked down at the whitewashed wood of the porch. There was a small spot where the wood started to split, and she could see the ground below it. She experienced a slight wooziness, as if she was standing on the deck of a docked ship.

The woman opened the door wearing linen shorts and an untucked button-up. The shirt was long, and for a moment, Mallory thought the woman wasn't wearing any pants at all. She looked back nervously at the taxi driver, but he had already pulled away.

Mallory handed the wine bottle to the woman. It was smudged with her clammy handprint. The woman smiled as she received it.

"It's German," said Mallory.

"It is," said the woman. "It's sweet."

Taking off her shoes as she stepped into the house, Mallory imagined she was becoming a character in one of the woman's books.

The house was only one level, plus a basement, but appeared almost palatial. To the right of the foyer, Mallory could see a long hallway with four other doors. To the left was a sitting area. This led into a dining room with a rosewood cabinet full of fine china, which looked identical to the one Mallory's mother had kept and never opened.

The foyer at the front of the house gave way to a kitchen, into which Mallory followed the woman. After popping the Riesling's cork, the woman poured two glasses. There would be no tour. She drained her glass and refilled it before Mallory sipped hers. "It's sweet," the woman said again, and now Mallory wondered whether the first time she'd said it was sweet related to the thoughtfulness of bringing the wine or the bottle's actual contents.

Dinner, which the woman cooked, was tofu stir-fry. They ate seated side by side on stools at the kitchen counter. It felt nice to be close and not have to look at one another. But all that was in view was a picture of the woman and a man—her husband—hanging on the fridge. The two of them were in hiking gear, standing on a cliff that overlooked a colorful seaside village, which the woman would later tell Mallory was part of Italy's Cinque Terre. In the photo, they looked sweaty and happy. Mallory had learned, when she looked the woman up online, that he was a full-time economics professor at the college but was away that semester guest lecturing at a school in the Midwest.

For almost two decades, he had worked as a financial analyst on Wall Street, while the woman had worked as a copywriter at an advertising agency. After they got married, they became dissatisfied with performing jobs that felt at once life-or-death and largely insignificant. They both chose to pursue things that would make them happier. For the woman, it was children's books. For her husband, it was teaching, though he too had written a book. Mallory had learned all this not from the woman herself but from the internet. The husband had published an op-ed a few years earlier called "Why I Left Wall Street." He had worked at Lehman Brothers. This was a name Mallory heard often that semester and would make him seem increasingly like a villain.

Between bites of food, Mallory obscured her mouth with the back of her hand. "This is so good," she told the woman. "Do you cook a lot?"

"When I have to," said the woman. "I'm a vegetarian. It's easier for me to cook for myself."

"I didn't know you were a vegetarian."

"How would you?"

Mallory gulped her wine. The imprint of her lips gummed the glass's rim. She asked the woman when she stopped eating meat.

Before emigrating, the woman said, her father had worked at a military outpost in Kaiserslautern, in Germany, where he met and befriended a group of American men whom he sometimes made food for and who goaded him to do so professionally. When he arrived in America, he opened a deli in New York. The woman's mother worked there, too; she made sandwiches and sold them out of the storefront window. They both came home smelling like pork, and the woman lost her taste for meat.

The woman went on: "My parents were very stingy and made spending even the smallest amounts of money seem catastrophic. At the supermarket, my father would go through every single container of prepackaged food, since the cost was determined by weight, to find the cheapest one available. This is a man who would put back a five-dollar package of chicken breasts in favor of one that cost four-ninety-nine, or stand with one plum in each of his palms to feel which one was lighter. So, whenever we went out to eat, which was not very often, I would order something that didn't have meat because these dishes were cheaper. I was always worried about being a financial burden on them."

"That's very noble," said Mallory. She knew how it was to feel like a burden on one's parents.

"Is it? It's not a very good way to live."

"Does your dad still run the shop?"

"No," said the woman. "He now manages a couple grocery stores upstate."

When they first moved to America, the woman said, they had lived in a part of Manhattan's Upper East Side called Yorkville, which housed a lot of the city's middle-class Germans. A little less than a decade after her father opened his deli, however, her sister became sick. They moved into a duplex in the Hudson Valley, the other half of which was inhabited by her aunt and uncle. He had to sell the deli.

To relay the information about her sister in this dispassionate way, Mallory saw, seemed to discourage follow-up questions. Mallory wondered whether the sister survived. She wondered whether she herself would eventually learn to dispatch the fact of her mother's death without sentiment. She could not even think of it now without gasping. Despite the drawn-out nature of her mother's illness, the death had come as a shock; it still shocked her, as if she was in a constant state of waking suddenly in a dark room.

Mallory was almost glad she didn't have to ask about the woman's sister. Doing so might invite a conversation during which she'd have to reveal her own loss. She did not want to tax the woman, whose patience seemed thin and whose interest she had somehow captured, with her grief. She did not want to seem complicated. So she said nothing.

After dinner, the woman washed the dishes. Mallory offered to help, but the woman waved her off. Watching the woman meticulously scrub between the tines of the forks, Mallory began to worry that appearing too young would cause the woman trepidation, so to make conversation she asked if the woman had seen any good movies lately. The woman laughed and shook her head.

Mallory blushed. She didn't know whether that meant she hadn't seen any or if the question itself was dumb.

The woman held up and reviewed a newly washed bowl. "My mother once made my father sleep on the couch for a week because she caught him cleaning only the tops of the plates. Apparently, this was how he'd washed them whenever he was asked to do it. She accused him of slowly poisoning us. After that, I started volunteering to do the dishes every night. I remember thinking, 'Let me do this for you.'"

She directed this last part at Mallory, who smiled, though the woman had recited these details with an offhandedness that suggested she'd recounted them many times before, which made Mallory worry she was wasting the woman's time and also that she herself was not special in hearing them. Another part of her, however, was glad the woman revealed anything to her at all. Mallory enjoyed listening to the woman talk. It was as if a layer had been peeled back from the universe's shell, and Mallory saw what lay underneath it.

When the woman finished with the dishes, they moved into the living room. The living room had a single sofa and floor-to-ceiling windows, which revealed an outdoor patio and an in-ground pool. The room's openness made Mallory feel delightfully small, as if whatever happened here would not matter to the outside world.

The woman sat down on the couch. She motioned for Mallory to sit beside her. Mallory, in the midst of a sip, did as she was instructed. Some of the wine splashed up as she sat, and her upper lip became slick with it.

On the couch, she was so close to the woman that she could smell her. It was a pleasantly acrid scent, like a bouquet of roses on the cusp of decay. The woman gulped down another glass of wine. After setting the empty glass down on the end table beside the couch, she said, "I might have gone with a Gewürztraminer."

Hearing the woman say something German, a daffy smile spread across Mallory's mouth. Before she could ask what the word was, the woman said, "What can I do for you? How can I help you?"

"Help me?"

"I want you to do well in life. You're smart and you have a wonderful laugh. When you laugh, I want to laugh, too."

"That's nice to hear."

"I mean it. It's lovely."

"I'd love to learn how to draw and write like you. I love your work so much."

"Oh," said the woman. "That's nice of you to say."

"This is fine, though," said Mallory, gesturing back and forth between them. "This is lovely." Trying on the woman's words felt false.

"I have an actor friend who practices saying 'It's an honor just to be nominated' in the mirror for thirty minutes every morning. He says it all different ways until it sounds sincere. It's part of his daily routine."

Mallory laughed, but then stopped herself short. "Now that I'm aware of my laugh, I'm not sure I like the sound of it. But I'm glad you do."

They looked at each other for a moment without saying anything. Almost absentmindedly, the woman reached out and started to twine a tress of Mallory's hair between two of her fingers. Mallory felt herself start to sweat. She hadn't believed her pursuit might ever bear fruit. She was embarrassed, as if she'd written an intense journal entry that she now had to read aloud. She looked away. In the corner of the room, the waxy leaves of a fake potted tree were ruffled by the breeze from an air-conditioning vent.

She felt she should say something, so she asked, "Have you always known you wanted to make children's books?"

The woman stopped touching Mallory's hair. Mallory felt both a brief relief and desire for the woman to touch her again. Something passed over the woman's face, the slight dimming of a light. She told Mallory about how she'd started writing and drawing in grade school, sitting in the corner of the classroom or under a tree on the playground, drawing herself talking and playing with the other children, whom she was too afraid to speak to in real life. "On paper," the woman said now, "everything could be safely contained." She said this with the same cadence she had used in the interview Mallory watched on You-Tube.

Mallory soured at the woman's canned answer. She must have looked visibly bitter, because the woman asked her what was wrong.

"I looked you up," Mallory said. "You said the same thing to PBS."

"Oh, I see," said the woman. "You'd like a response that is just for you."

"I would love that."

"I wanted to be an actress," the woman said. "I felt that I would be good at being someone else. But I spent so much time as a child by myself that I wanted people to know who I was. I had all these bizarre thoughts and was desperate to know if anyone else shared them. Besides, I was not pretty enough to act."

"That can't be true," said Mallory. "I mean, you are."

The woman's weary eyes went wide. She inched closer to Mallory and leaned forward to initiate what Mallory thought was a kiss. Instead, the woman rested her forehead on Mallory's. The tips of their noses touched. This felt impossibly, almost unbearably intimate. The woman's breath smelled of peppers and soy sauce, and for years Mallory would associate this taste with this moment. The woman said, "You can kiss me if you'd like."

To have her wants understood without articulating them herself, and to have those desires be accepted and even encouraged, made Mallory feel bold enough to place her lips on the woman's. She had only kissed a girl once before, and she was excited and relieved to be doing it with a woman she so admired. Mallory felt a moment of becoming exactly the thing she had suspected she was; more than resignation, there came a sense of *Yes, that's it*. It was like hearing one of those German words that encapsulated a complex set of emotions.

She and the woman kissed for a while, passing one kiss back and forth until it became so large they'd have to stop. It was, thought Mallory, the opposite of sharing a joint.

Breathless, the woman drew away. With her eyes closed, she ran a thumb over her own lips. "I haven't been kissed like that in a long time."

They sat in silence for several seconds. Mallory became both hungry and afraid of her hunger, as if she were at an important banquet with a lavish meal before her that would nonetheless appear rude to consume.

Disquieted by the silence, Mallory picked up the woman's hand and held it. On the inside of the woman's wrist was a slight constellation of wounds. When she was young, the woman said, she'd been bitten by a dog. She said, "Would you believe it was a German Shepherd?"

Mallory told the woman that, on her, the same spot felt good when kissed. She told the woman that, when she was younger, she would sit in the bathroom stalls at school and kiss herself there, dreaming her wrist was someone else's lips. Saying this, however, she became embarrassed at how alone she had been then. The woman took Mallory's wrist and kissed it twice.

"Don't make me go back," Mallory said.

"I can't make you do anything," the woman said. She looked past Mallory into the kitchen and stared at the microwave clock. Then she took her cell phone from the end table and looked at it, as if she did not believe the other clock. "But it is late."

A few days later, on a Tuesday, Mallory walked by the woman's office. She wasn't sure she should go in. They hadn't seen or spoken to one another, even through email, since the dinner, and the office felt like a strange place to acknowledge a kiss. Also, Mallory worried that the woman wouldn't acknowledge it at all, or would say it was a mistake, and Mallory would be forced to go back to her ordinary life.

Still, she knocked on the door. The woman waved her in and said, "I imagine you want that door closed."

Mallory shut it and went to sit next to the woman's desk. It might have looked, to someone walking by, as if Mallory was there for a polygraph test. "Sorry," she said. "I shouldn't have just shown up like this."

"You're not sorry."

Mallory blinked. "I wanted to see you."

"It's fine," said the woman. "I'm glad you did. No one comes to see me."

"You know, on your Rate My Professors page, one of your

former students said that it's easy to get an A if they show up to your office hours."

"It's true, and still no one comes."

Most students who took her children's literature course wanted to be teachers, the woman said, and she lamented how little interest they had in seeing the stories as works of art, as ends in and of themselves rather than simply as a means of instruction. She lectured Mallory on their craft, how picture books are lessons in how to tell stories without exposition or flashbacks; how a sentence written for children only does a single thing; and how the verb "to feel," which gets short shrift in literature, is the most effective way to convey raw emotion.

The woman, Mallory realized, was glad to have a rapt audience. What the woman liked most about teaching, it seemed, was that people paid to listen to her, to have her opinions pressed upon them. The woman wanted to be someone of whom others asked questions and from whom they sought answers. That the woman had an enormous ego—that any woman had an ego like that, something Mallory wasn't sure she'd seen before—delighted her.

Sensing that the woman wanted some sort of praise, but also believing that she was not looking for a response to her brief lecture, Mallory thanked her for the other night. "For the dinner," she said, "and the conversation."

"It was nice," the woman said.

"It was. I'm glad you invited me."

The woman smiled. She leaned back in her seat. "I had lunch with a friend a few days ago, a pediatric oncologist. I've known her for years, and she is very dear to me. She ordered a salad with dressing on the side, and when it came out, there was dressing all over it. She said to the waiter, 'I'm sorry, I wanted it on the side,' and the waiter brought her a little plastic cup filled with extra dressing, which he then spilled on the table. At the end of the meal, my friend tipped him twenty percent. I couldn't believe it." Incredulous, the woman shook her head. "I looked at her and thought, 'You are a good person, and we have nothing in common.'"

The woman laughed at her own joke, and Mallory did, too, though she was a little fearful of the woman in that moment, of what seemed to be the woman's capacity for meanness. But the woman's life—both of their lives—had been marked by a kind of hardness, and Mallory wondered whether the way to offset that hardness was to refract it back onto the world. She told the woman, "I think you and I have a lot in common."

⁍

On Thursday, the woman invited Mallory back to her house. She poured the two of them a glass of red wine. It was just after four, the time when they usually went to the gym. Nervous, Mallory had not eaten lunch that afternoon, and even just a single sip of wine made her weak-kneed. The woman too looked woozy, as if she'd been drinking before Mallory got there.

Mallory took a sip and told the woman she liked her blouse. This was not an empty compliment; Mallory really did like the shirt. It was a white collared top with black polka dots. Mallory thought she could see herself in such a shirt—she didn't really know how to dress professionally—and hoped the woman would reveal where she'd bought it.

The woman said, "It's handmade chiffon."

"Where did you get it?"

"On the rue des Veaux, in Strasbourg."

"Where's that?"

"On the border of France and Germany."

Aloud, Mallory repeated the name in hopes of committing it to memory: "rue des Veaux, in Strasbourg." Her saying it lacked the charm of the woman's accent. She asked the woman, "Do you travel a lot?"

"I love it," said the woman. "It's my favorite thing in the world."

They talked about where the woman had traveled: Zagreb, Bali, Bora Bora. As the woman spoke about her vacations, her speech sped up, as if she had just returned and needed to recount the details quickly before she forgot them.

One of her favorite places she had visited, she told Mallory, was Cinque Terre, where she had gone because she loved a kind of liqueur called limoncello and wanted to tour a vineyard that made it. As she told Mallory this, she stuck her thumb toward the picture of the seaside village on her fridge, the one with her husband, as if to suggest their having gone there together was almost incidental. Since she and the woman kissed, Mallory had started reading his book on market psychology; whenever she read a passage she thought was smart or fascinating, she'd toss the book across the room.

The woman and her husband—"we" was her only acknowledgment of him—spent most summers traveling to different places. She asked Mallory if she'd like to see. Mallory wanted to see anything the woman wanted to show her. She wanted to see the whole world the way the woman did.

The woman left the kitchen and came back with a short stack of photo books. She arrayed them on the counter like a child revealing her rock collection. She looked sheepish and vulnerable all of a sudden, but eager and hopeful too, and Mallory realized that the woman needed her to feel the same way about the pictures as she did, that they contained some kind of magic. Flipping through them, Mallory did feel that way; they were evidence of a life wonderfully, glamorously lived.

The pictures were of flora and fauna, of monuments and oceans, of the interiors and exteriors of religious sites, of rolling hills and empty hotel rooms, and not one of them had a single human being in the frame.

"Oh, wow," said Mallory. "But where are you?"

"Me?" The woman said this as if it was preposterous to keep photographs of herself. *How was it*, Mallory wondered with tipsy astonishment, *that the woman could be self-centered but not vain?*

"There aren't any people in these pictures."

"Yes," the woman said, "isn't it wonderful?"

Each page was labeled with the name of the place where the pictures were taken. Mallory said, "Where even is Seychelles?" She pronounced it "see-chel-iss."

"Say-shells," the woman said, putting her hand on Mallory's cheek.

Mallory held it there, closing her eyes, thinking how good the woman's hand felt on her face. She brushed her lips across the woman's wrist, and when she opened her eyes, she saw the woman's were now closed. Worried that whatever window had just opened would snap shut if she did nothing, Mallory kissed the woman on the lips. They continued to kiss while standing in the kitchen, their hands resting on one another's waists. The woman kissed the same way she wrote: tender and terse. The economy of the kisses left Mallory wet with want.

When Mallory pulled away, she was panting. She put her face into the crook of the woman's neck and whispered, "Can we do this somewhere else?"

The woman brought Mallory to her bedroom. Once inside, she pressed the door shut behind them and said, "This is what you want, right?" It was as if she was offering Mallory the whole room. It was a nice room, with a big king-sized bed.

Mallory moved to sit on the bed, but the woman stopped her. Clothes worn outside the home carried germs, the woman said.

The woman began taking off her own clothes, and Mallory did the same. After she took off her sweater and jeans, Mallory folded them and laid them neatly on a chair beside the bureau.

Her eyes fell on the woman's body. There were stark tan lines where a swimsuit had been, which gave Mallory the impression of uncovering something that had been kept hidden. She looked away, but the woman told her to look, so she did. For years, Mallory had stopped herself from looking at women with lust, but now the woman wanted just that.

The two of them sat beside one another on the bed. They were facing a window, but a thick lace curtain obscured what lay beyond it. Mallory turned toward the woman and kissed the woman's shoulder, her neck, her lips. They kissed for a while before the woman went to lie back on the bed, reaching her hand into her underwear to rub herself, soft and slow. Her eyes were closed. Mallory, still seated beside the woman but looking down at her, understood that the woman wanted to be watched doing this too, so that was what Mallory did: watched.

Almost as a reflex, Mallory, who'd taught herself to masturbate by watching other women do it in porn, began to mirror the woman's movements on herself. She felt her own wetness and fell back next to the woman. The two of them moved like this, alone and together. Their breaths became heavier and heavier until the woman whispered, "Do you want to touch me?" Mallory said yes, and the woman took Mallory's hand in hers, bringing it between her legs. The woman, using Mallory's hand to rub herself, opened her legs wider, and Mallory sat up to kneel between them. A low moan trembled in the woman's throat. The woman removed her own hand and Mallory continued. "Yes," the woman said. "Like that." It was if she was teaching Mallory how to draw.

Mallory put her hand on the woman's heart and felt it beat faster and faster until the woman shut her legs, pushing Mallory's hand away. Mallory continued to kiss the woman's neck. She snatched the woman's hand and stuck it between her own legs. Letting out a little laugh, the woman did just as Mallory had done.

Despite having had sex before, Mallory had never come in front of someone else, and now she felt very open, as if something had been taken from her. It was a pleasant feeling. Being emptied this way by the woman meant she was no longer, for the moment, filled with grief. Other than the light-headed self-indulgence of someone who'd gotten her way, she'd had hardly any thoughts at all.

They lay quiet for a while before the woman went to take a shower. She put on a pair of rubber flip-flops she kept next to the bed and walked naked to the nearby bathroom. Mallory lay in bed with her hands between her legs, wallowing in her body's hot, wet throb. A few minutes later, the woman emerged, wrapped snugly in a fluffy bathrobe tied at the waist.

Mallory fantasized that the two of them were on vacation together. "I like your robe," she said.

"I stole it from the St. Regis in Mexico City," the woman said. "Don't tell anyone."

Mallory laughed. She said, "I won't."

Mallory would go to the woman's house whenever the woman wanted. Every time the woman invited Mallory over, Mallory felt as though the woman was doing her a favor. This was partly because each time, the woman would pay for her taxi ride back to campus and typically gave Mallory more than the fare.

They had sex slowly, their bodies close together, and afterwards, they pulled the sheets over their heads, gifting each other greedy, languorous glances. It made Mallory happy to be and be seen naked, to desire and be desired in a way that was only possible in private. The warm, breathy silence and the caul of the comforter made it feel as though they were sealed off from the rest of the world. It was as if time and judgment did not exist. There was nothing and no one else.

Lying in such proximity, Mallory would watch the woman and wonder, *Why me?* This led her to wonder, *Who are you?* Mallory could have dug more forcefully into the woman's life, but she didn't. Though she was curious, mostly she did not want to be a bother. Also, not asking about what the woman's life was like now allowed Mallory to forget that the woman's fingernails, painted pastel pink, belonged to someone more than twice her age. She could look around the woman's bedroom and forget it was shared with someone else.

In bed, though, the woman asked Mallory questions about her life and nodded her head thoughtfully at the answers. The woman listened to Mallory calmly and deliberately, often, it seemed, waiting for Mallory to say something interesting. Mallory became conscious of summoning only the details from her life that were unusual or arresting, like her childhood hamster that had died, of all things, from pinkeye, or her having been a small-time drug dealer in high school. That Mallory was reciting only the fascinating things about her life, minus the mundane details and the too-big wounds, made her feel as though she was a purely fascinating person.

She told the woman that she had only one ovary, which was true. Because of a cyst, the other had had to be removed when she was two. Mallory believed this was interesting—both tragic and droll. The woman was drawing with her finger on Mallory's naked belly. She asked, "Can you have children?"

"I don't know," said Mallory. "I don't think I want kids, anyway. Do you?"

"I wouldn't have made a very good parent. I wouldn't have known how."

"Were yours bad?"

"Not at all," the woman said. "Sometimes I feel so much affection for them, especially my mother, that I feel like I might cry. She was happy in Germany and has been much less pleased with her life here. I don't think she's been truly happy ever since. There were whole years of my childhood that, when I look back at them, were devoted to trying to make her smile. I remember reading about Sisyphus as a teenager and thinking, 'Hey, that's me.'"

"What is she like?" Mallory asked.

"Kooky," the woman said. She became starry-eyed, smiling widely in a way that surprised Mallory. "She is someone who goes to church every Sunday, volunteers there, but will curse anyone who talks to her before she's had her second cup of coffee. She will lick food off her fingers but cannot touch doorknobs or light switches—even in her own home—with her bare hand."

This last thing was a habit the woman shared—Mallory had noticed that the woman always used her shirt to open doors—and Mallory wondered if there was anything like that she herself had picked up from her own mother.

The woman spoke about her mother with a tenderness that made Mallory envious. She too loved her mother but often could only recall her being depressed and sick in bed. Her mother had gotten sick when Mallory was ten, and again when she was thirteen, and spent the years of remission fearful of getting sick again, which was ultimately what happened. Mallory's father had become so preoccupied with her mother's health that he too had kind of disappeared. Thinking this way, Mallory saw herself as a child born of two ghosts.

"You're a good daughter," she told the woman. "Your mom must know how much you love her."

"We both do the best with what we've been given."

"Me and you?"

"I'm sure you are a good daughter, too."

Mallory didn't answer but appreciated the woman's use of the present tense.

�™

Many things reminded Mallory of sex: the smooth underside of her classroom desk, the taste and texture of baby carrots, water from a faucet falling onto her fingers, a whiff of sweat from her armpit, the slap of bare feet on the bathroom floor. The world felt alive to her in a way it hadn't before. It felt as though the earth itself knew about their affair, but no one living on it did.

At the gym, she and the woman pretended never to have met. Mallory would show up first, and when the woman arrived, she would get onto the treadmill in front of Mallory. Unable to help herself, Mallory would stare at the woman's ass, punch-drunk from having seen it bare.

Sometimes, as she ran, Mallory fantasized about what it would be like to confront the woman in the crowded gym and expose their affair. She had an improbable advantage over the woman, who had so much to lose—her marriage, her job at the college, her publishing career—while Mallory had nothing. The best part of having nothing, Mallory thought, was that it couldn't be lost.

One afternoon, because she had stayed up the previous night studying, Mallory became tired before she hit her usual two miles. She went into the locker room and sat down on a wooden bench in front of her locker. Bleary-eyed, she looked down at her body, more fit than it had ever been before. She got turned on by the sight of herself. *Everything good that will happen in my life*, she thought, *will happen because of this woman*.

A few minutes later, as Mallory was lifting her shirt and poking at her belly, the woman walked in.

Silently, the woman got herself a shower towel before opening her locker. Her eyes shifted to regard Mallory peripherally. During this clandestine look, the woman, who was still breathing heavily from her workout, began taking off her clothes. First, she took off her shirt, then her leggings, then her sports bra, and finally, her underwear. The woman stood naked for a moment before wrapping a towel around herself.

Mallory realized this was how the woman was: she at once withheld and invited. The woman fulfilled so many of Mallory's wants but left so many wants unfulfilled that the feeling of wanting in and of itself became desirable. There was an untouchable intensity, or an intense untouchability, to keeping a secret, to having a continuous crush, that Mallory wanted never to lose.

As the woman turned to get into the shower, she walked by and cupped her hand on Mallory's shoulder. Mallory looked up, but before she could meet the woman's gaze, the woman moved past her.

Whenever she wasn't with the woman, Mallory was by herself in the library. She believed she had to be alone, since solitude was what made her available to the woman in the first place.

There were times when her relationship with the woman made her feel invincible, as if it created a force field around her, and other times, particularly with Joy, when she felt the bewildering shock of a bubble's pop.

Coming back from the woman's house one evening, Mallory found Joy clipping her toenails while on the phone with her boyfriend. She was wearing his overlarge UConn sweatshirt. Seeing Mallory in the doorway, Joy mouthed an apology. Mallory waved it off. Surely, Mallory thought, he must have heard those hideous snips. It seemed he didn't care.

Mallory couldn't imagine doing such a thing in front of the woman. With the woman, Mallory had the endless sense of teetering on an edge; she was always on her best behavior. She expended a lot of energy on what to say and do. Mostly, she enjoyed this feeling, an extreme carefulness, like drawing without an eraser and with only one piece of paper.

After ending the call, Joy said, "I hate the sound of someone else clipping their nails." She gave a playacted shudder. "Sorry."

Mallory pointed at Joy's cell phone. "He didn't seem to mind."

"He's seen and heard so much worse."

"That must be nice."

"Any day now, I'm half expecting him to say, 'You know what, Jessica doesn't clip her toenails when I'm with her.'"

Jessica was one of the many girls back home Joy believed was interested in her boyfriend. She named the others. Doing this made her so upset that Mallory started to dislike those girls too, even as she realized she herself was like them, pursuing someone who was not hers. She felt a little guilty.

Joy and her boyfriend were high school sweethearts, as Mallory's parents had been. When she thought about this, Mallory toggled between jealousy and pity.

"I think it's just so much easier to go after someone in a relationship," Joy said. "Think about it: When you go after someone in a relationship, all you have to do is be better than the person they're in the relationship with. If you're going after someone single, you have to be better than literally everyone else."

Mallory laughed and laid back in her bed. She felt stoned, though she hadn't smoked pot in months. From where she was, she could see the book by the woman's husband on her desk. He was smarter, wealthier, older, and a man. *In what way*, Mallory wondered, *was she better than him?*

༝

On a Friday night, a week before they were to leave for Thanksgiving and one week after Mallory's nineteenth birthday, Joy brought Mallory to an off-campus party. It was a "stoplight" party: if single, you wore green; if taken, you wore red; if unsure, yellow. Mallory put on the same kelly-green sweater she had worn the night she first went to the woman's house, though she did not feel single and was uninterested, she thought, in meeting someone else.

When she'd told the woman she was going, the woman had said, *Go, live your life.* The woman asked, *Who would wear yellow?* She did not, however, tell the woman it had been her birthday. She thought the woman would not care that she was now nineteen instead of eighteen.

At the party, Mallory stayed close to Joy. She admired the way Joy moved seamlessly between topics of conversation. Despite having taken AP government and US history in high school, Mallory had little understanding of the country and the world at large, and she dithered when people talked about politics or what was in the news. It was as if, after having taken the exams last year, she had let all the information go. She had already forgotten about senate confirmations and what an attorney general did. The only things she could remember were the plots of the fiction she'd read.

A large group gathered to discuss the final presidential debate that had taken place at their school just a month earlier. They talked about a man named Joe who was a plumber, and Mallory had difficulty discerning whether this man was real or not so stayed quiet. Two weeks before the party, the country had elected a Black president. Mallory had been spending so much time with the woman—and anticipating their next meeting when they weren't together—that she hadn't thought of anything else;

although local and international newspapers had lain on her kitchen counter, the woman hadn't ever brought up politics. Mallory had not realized the gravity of the election until she'd heard and spoken of it aloud now with her classmates. That the world was shifting in this significant way made her feel intoxicated. Yet part of her smarted that the world continued to spin regardless of her mother.

Mallory must have looked dazed, because Joy yanked on her sleeve. "What's up?"

"America did this really big thing," Mallory said.

"They don't get the news in Narnia?"

Mallory rolled her eyes, laughed.

"That's where you go, right?"

"Right, yeah."

"Our closets must be bigger than I thought."

"I'm mostly in the library. It's nothing exciting."

Joy pinched at Mallory's green sweater. "Then you have more work than me."

Joy went to get the two of them another round of drinks. Alone, Mallory looked around. Toward the corner of the room, two boys were egging on a third to talk to a pretty girl. A rap song rumbled from a tall subwoofer. The speaker was connected to a Mac laptop that lay open on the ground, and someone walking by nearly trampled it. She envied the careless way in which her peers appeared to live. She felt at once much older than them and much younger.

A girl with short brown hair was by the speaker, stroking the strap of her leather shoulder bag. There was another girl in a floral-print dress and combat boots flicking the tab of a beer can with her tongue. She had thought her relationship with the woman shielded her from desiring anyone else but found now that this wasn't true. Being with the woman felt like standing underneath an awning during a downpour, but it would always continue to rain.

The girl in the dress looked back at her. They smiled at each other. Mallory wondered what it would be like to be in a relationship with her, a girl her own age, but she had no examples of that. She wondered what it would be like to have sex with her but then worried that, just looking at each other, the girl would know what Mallory was thinking about. She felt a little perverted and, thinking about the woman, more than a little disloyal. She looked away from the girl and waited for Joy.

Joy came back and handed Mallory a beer. A loveseat opened up, and they moved to fill it. The couch was so short that Joy sat with her legs draped over Mallory's lap. Joy sighed and smiled. She was happy and drunk. "You're lucky," she said. "I used to look forward to a new school year because it always felt like a redo, like a fresh start. I wish I wasn't so attached to my life back home."

Mallory was not attached. She realized then that Joy's anxiety over the possibility of her boyfriend cheating was also fear of her own wandering eye. Joy, whom Mallory considered prettier and smarter and more personable, envied Mallory's unattachment. There was nothing else in the world other than Mallory's aloneness that could make her the object of Joy's envy.

A day before Thanksgiving, Mallory took the train to New Jersey to see her father. He picked her up at the station, and when she saw him, she was struck by how much the affair would hurt him. That she was sleeping with a married woman closer to his age than her own was an act of such deviancy that she had the sense of having been parted from her previous life completely. Now, in the car, he called her "kiddo," which felt unendurably gracious, like being given a gift by someone she hadn't bought anything for.

They ordered a pizza and watched an action movie. This had been an almost nightly routine for the two of them—takeout and a cheesy film—just after her mother died. Explosions, car chases, the whole world in peril, food prepared by someone else. It had saved them. They spent just as long picking apart the movies' plot holes as they did watching the films themselves, even ones they liked. They'd laugh at the hack writing and come up with myriad other ways the stories could have been told. Later, however, Mallory would feel bad about making fun of how the movie was written, of the person who wrote it, knowing how hard it was to take what was in one's head and get it out into the world.

After the movie, her father kissed her on the forehead and went upstairs to his room. She sat on the sofa, stumped, not knowing whether he was happy to see her or if she was a reminder of what he'd lost. They'd hardly talked about what happened. At times, Mallory was comforted by this; her grief was her own, and she could do with it what she wanted.

Mallory went from room to room turning all the lights on and off, and then went down into the basement, where her mother's piano was. On top of the piano were photographs of her mother, most of them taken before Mallory was ten; after her mother had lost her hair from the first round of chemotherapy, she stopped wanting to be in pictures. Some of them were of her mother in high school, some with her sister, Mallory's aunt, who—with her paler complexion and wavy hair—Mallory now resembled.

There was one taken at Mallory's grandmother's condo in Fort Lauderdale. In it, Mallory was six or seven. Her father stood in the complex's swimming pool, and she stood on his shoulders, her fists balled and her arms outstretched, like a cheerleader without pom-poms. Mallory's mother sat by the edge of the pool, facing the camera. In the photo, she was beautiful in an arcane way. Because it was a Polaroid, the blue of the water was now golden from weathering and age. It was Mallory's aunt, also dead, who had taken the picture. Looking at it now, she felt as though she was knocking on a locked door with no one on the other side.

Mallory sat at the piano bench. She used to sit on her mother's lap while her mother played, but she had never picked up any of the songs herself. She wanted to ask her mother what it was like to lose a sister, to fall in love. She wanted to ask her mother lots of things.

✧

They spent Thanksgiving with Mallory's maternal grandmother, Ruth. Because Mallory's father was not Jewish, Ruth, who was, had always offered him only a halfhearted tolerance. The feeling was mutual. She had always demonstrated a preference for Mallory's aunt, her other daughter, over Mallory's mother. At the funeral for Mallory's aunt, who had died a decade before Mallory's mother, Ruth had turned to Mallory's father and said through tears, "God took the wrong daughter."

Before Mallory's aunt became sick, the family—Mallory, her parents, her grandmother, her aunt and uncle—had spent a few weeks every summer in Fort Lauderdale. Some nights, Ruth took Mallory to play bingo with the other tenants. The two of them would gossip during the lulls between games; the other tenants, who were more or less deaf, couldn't hear a word. It was exhilarating for Mallory to be so openly odious. Her grandmother told her stories of a suspected jewelry thief in the complex who had wormed his way into the bedrooms of naïve women in order to steal their possessions. "Let this be a lesson," her grandmother had said. "If you crack your door open for someone even just a smidge, you can bet that door will be pushed all the way open."

Then, one year, her grandmother had a stroke. It happened while she was on an elevator, alone. Afterward, she doubled down on her mistrust of everyone around her. This hatred, Mallory's father often said, was what sustained and nourished her.

Ruth lived now in a neighborhood with houses rented mostly by local college students. Ringing her doorbell, Mallory saw her family as strange, as if they were three unrelated actors playing roles on a television show. Her grandmother took a long time to open the door.

"Well," Ruth said through the screen, "look who it is. You look an awful lot like a granddaughter I had."

Mallory laughed. "How are you?"

"Oh, hanging on."

Mallory's father said, "It beats the alternative."

Her grandmother said, "Does it?"

All this took place before she let Mallory and her father into the house. This was by design; if anyone was walking or driving by, they would see that she had visitors.

Ruth hung no family photos in her house. On the wall along a small stairway leading to the second floor—which she had to crawl on in order to ascend—she had hung a portrait of herself when she was much, much younger.

The three of them ate gravlax in between bursts of small talk. Ruth asked how school was going and if Mallory had met any boys. "I've met tons of them," Mallory said.

"I bet," said her grandmother. "You've become a woman, finally. You're wearing your hair down, and you've lost weight."

"I've been going to the gym."

Ruth turned to Mallory's father and jabbed a finger at his chest. "What about you?"

"I haven't been going to the gym," he said.

"It's been months. You're only a man."

Mallory's father waved this off in a dismissive way that made Mallory think dating was on his mind all the time. She wondered how long he'd been thinking of other women, if this had begun while her mother was still in the hospital—if the promise of another life lessened the loss of the old one.

After dinner, as her father did the dishes, Mallory sat on the couch next to her grandmother. They watched television, though Ruth could not find a program that interested her. Finally, she put on a game show and set the remote aside. She sat slumped on the edge of the sofa, her body vibrating with anxiety, as if she couldn't wait to be alone. She kept glancing at the thin-strapped watch that hung loosely on her wrist. Often, she'd complained that no one called or visited, but whenever someone did, she appeared not to enjoy the company. Mallory thought she understood this: her grandmother wanted something so much that to have it felt off. Feeling a swell of affection for her, Mallory tried to rest her head on her grandmother's shoulder, but it was bony and unforgiving. "What are you doing?" her grandmother asked.

Ruth got up from the couch to smoke a Pall Mall on the front porch. She could barely stand and had lost two daughters to cancer; this made her cigarette habit seem absurd and brazen. Mallory watched her body shake as she smoked, wondering if the only way to allay the strange slant of one's life was to embrace it.

They left just as it started getting dark. In the car on the way home, Mallory asked her father about Ruth's life. Her first husband had been in the army, and when he deployed to Korea, she shacked up with someone else. When he returned safely from the war, she annulled their marriage. Her second husband,

Mallory's grandfather, died unremarkably just before Mallory was born. Her third husband had become ill, and instead of staying by his side, she went to Fort Lauderdale for vacation. He died while she sunned herself by the pool. He died while she lived her life. She'd had a long life and had given herself the chance to live it. Mallory's father spoke about her with such disdain, but in hearing about her selfishness, Mallory felt closer to her than ever before. Mallory thought, *She's just like me.*

That night, in her childhood bed, Mallory watched a movie on her laptop. The characters' unhappiness was due partly to a family curse. After the movie finished, she shut her computer and tried to fall asleep. She kept picturing her grandmother's varicose veins, the same veins that had snaked up her mother's legs and would most likely mark her own one day.

Mallory felt sorry for her grandmother; the amount of loss in her life exceeded what Mallory herself could imagine. In addition to three husbands and a sister, she had lost both her daughters. She had also fallen out with the few friends she'd had. Her disconnection from the world seemed designed to protect herself from further loss.

Mallory fell asleep imagining how she would recap what she had learned about her grandmother to the woman. The woman, she thought, would find it all delightful: Ruth's pitiless romantic history, her wicked insistence on living on her own terms.

Over the holiday, the woman had stayed with her parents in the Hudson Valley. It was, she told Mallory, the first time since she got married that she and her husband hadn't spent Thanksgiving together. Rather than fly home, he had decided to stay out west. "He's probably having an affair," the woman said. She said this with such nonchalance that Mallory wondered if they both regularly slept with other people.

They stood for a while in the kitchen. It was warm for the first day of December; the temperature was in the fifties. Mallory drank a glass of water and, when she was done, placed the glass on the counter and made a show of wiping her mouth with her shirt, exposing her stomach.

They looked at each other, and then the woman looked up at the ceiling, laughing to herself. Mallory knew the woman was happy to see her. With a surprising seriousness, she imagined their relationship as turning some sort of corner, true affection poking its neck out from the denuded bushes of lust. Briefly, she imagined the woman would leave her husband. As if to brag,

Mallory turned toward his image on the fridge, hanging just above a built-in icemaker.

She kissed the woman squarely on the lips. As they kissed, the woman cupped her hands around Mallory's face. Mallory felt as though her insides were liquid in a bowl from which the woman was taking a drink. Her body lifted toward the woman.

They went into the bedroom. After taking off her clothes, the woman sat on the bed with her back against the upholstered headboard. When Mallory was done undressing, she sat astride the woman. She rocked herself slowly in the woman's lap, tilting her head back so they weren't making eye contact. The speed with which Mallory rocked increased. It seemed that one or both of them might come from this, and once they took their underwear off, Mallory did. She gasped and pressed her face into the top of the woman's head, partly out of surprise that it had felt as good as it did.

Mallory peeled herself off the woman, who rolled to lie flat on her stomach. Mallory was now the one sitting up against the headboard. Her eyelids felt heavy, as if someone was standing on them. "Sorry," she said.

The woman's face was turned away, but Mallory saw her eyes were opened. One of the woman's arms dangled off the side of the bed. "Don't be. It was nice. I'm a little tired."

"Is everything okay?"

"I am always exhausted after I see my family."

"Do you still have family in Germany? Do you go back there a lot?"

The woman turned to face her. She wore a quizzical expression on her face, as if to say, *Is that what you're thinking about right now?* She rested her elbows on the bed and held her head up with her hands. Her legs were bent at the knee and crossed at the ankle. She looked like a girl gossiping at a slumber party. "Yes," said the woman, "I still have family there. Also, it is nice to leave America once in a while. So much here feels like a lie."

"Like what?"

"Americans smile too much, and it means so little. When a German person smiles, you know you have deserved it." She gave Mallory a ridiculous grin.

Mallory smiled back at her, so wide her cheeks hurt.

"Germany is a strange place," said the woman. "But of course, everyone says this about everywhere."

"What makes it strange?"

"We pretend what happened did not really happen. In order to move forward, we don't dwell on what came before."

"That makes sense. Who'd want to remember that?"

Sleepily, the woman thought about this. She took Mallory's hand and held it palm up. With the pad of her index finger, she began tracing the lines there, as if she were performing palmistry. "Shame and pride often feel like the same thing. You begin to want to protect even the most embarrassing parts of your life."

A moony quietude descended on the room.

"I felt so weird being home over break," Mallory said. "It was like the house had gotten smaller, or that I had gotten larger. I felt like Godzilla stomping around a tiny city."

"Why do you see yourself as a monster?"

"It's just that I've grown into this person that no one else has really seen."

"We do not change that much from who we are as children. Who you are now is who you always have been."

This struck Mallory as true. Lately, she felt less like she had become someone else than that she had become herself. It was, she thought, the woman who had allowed this to happen. "What were you like as a child?"

"Miserable," said the woman. The forthrightness with which she offered this frightened Mallory. The woman let the word sit there with them before getting out of the bed and putting on her rubber slippers. Mallory watched her walk into the bathroom.

Beguiled by the woman's dismal admission and wanting to occupy her mind until the woman's return, Mallory picked up a pen and paper from the nightstand next to her. It was the pad the woman used to jot down phone messages. There weren't any. Absently, she began to doodle on it, little shapes and faces. Whenever she was with the woman, she felt inspired, filled with the desire to document and create.

A few minutes later, the woman shut off the shower and came back into the bedroom. She took the pad from Mallory and ripped the page from the rest, smoothing her hand over the next page to see if Mallory's sketches had left any impressions.

"I once slept with a married man," the woman said. "I used to leave things like this around his house to see if his wife would find them."

"Did she?"

"That's what you want to know?" The woman asked this with a sly smile, as if she was teasing Mallory for being narrow-minded.

Mallory said, "I want to know anything you want to tell me."

The woman got back into the bed. She held out her hand to take the pen from Mallory, who lay naked, half-covered by the sheet.

The woman said, "My father used to take us to a Yankees game every year when we lived in the city. One year, my sister— we were twins—brought me into the bathroom stall at the stadium and showed me this heart-shaped stain on her chest." Here, the woman rubbed her own chest, as if the mark had once been on her. "It was a lupus rash. Do you know what that is?"

"Not really," Mallory lied. It was the disease House, the doctor on the television show of the same name, always thought his patients had. She did not want to reveal this was how she knew of it.

"Lupus is an autoimmune disorder," the woman said. "It weakens one's body and makes it difficult to fight off infection. She was constantly in and out of the hospital, and the apartment we lived in started to feel very small, so we moved upstate, where my parents still live now. This was where I stayed over the break."

"The duplex," Mallory said, to show the woman she had been listening, that she had remembered.

"The duplex," said the woman. "But my sister seemed to keep getting sicker, and it was hard to escape what was happening inside the house. By then, I was seventeen. I graduated from high school a year early and went to Barnard for college. I commuted there, though I would stay in the city as long as I could to avoid going home. I was so relieved to have the time to myself, even though I felt very lonely. One morning, on the train into Manhattan, I ran into a friend of my father's who lived near us in

Beacon but worked in the city. He kept a small apartment there, and soon we started sleeping together. For his job, he traveled all over, and he told me about all the glamorous things he saw. I remember thinking, 'I will have that life someday.' He learned that I liked to draw and brought me back these expensive pens from the countries he visited, which I used to doodle in class and at home, thrilled with the knowledge of how I had obtained them. I remember feeling so special. It was euphoric to be seen that way by someone like him. It was euphoric to be seen at all."

The woman smiled at this, tight-lipped and a little sad, and so Mallory did, too. But something inside Mallory cracked open. She wanted to tell the woman how grateful she was, how the woman's desire for her allayed a lifetime of feeling ugly, how euphoric it was to be seen by a woman like her.

There was also a lot she wanted to tell the woman about her own life: her mother's illness, for one, which sounded astonishingly similar to what the woman's sister went through. She and the woman shared so many of the same pains. That their childhoods had similarities gave Mallory the impression, upon looking at the woman nearly naked in the bed, that she was looking at some future form of herself.

Mallory laid her head in the woman's lap. "Is your sister okay?"

"She passed away last year."

"I'm sorry."

"She suffered for a long time."

"We really do have a lot in common," Mallory said. "What you're describing about your sister is sort of what happened to my mom."

"When was this?" the woman asked. She said it with a compassionate flatness that suggested she had already, in some sense, guessed.

"She died this past May. But I guess, like your sister, she was sick for a long time." Mallory paused. "It was the same disease Roald Dahl had," though she felt silly after adding this.

The woman smoothed Mallory's hair. "I appreciate you telling me. That kind of grief can be isolating, but it can be even harder to tell someone else."

"Yes," Mallory said. She had mentioned her mother's death only once to Joy, who had looked at her with a teeth-clenched discomfort, as if Joy, who was very close with her own mother, had seen in Mallory a ghastly prospect.

"When my sister was sick," the woman said, "I craved company. But when people were there, I would wish them away, as if they were intruding. Her being sick meant more to me than it did to them. It was like seeing other people peeking in through a window while I was trying to look out of it."

"It still feels that way."

"I know."

They eventually fell asleep in bed together, but when Mallory woke, she discovered the woman was in her office with the door closed. Mallory stood by the door and listened. The woman was talking on the phone. "I don't know what I'll have," she said. "I'm tired. Maybe I'll order something." She said, "I miss you." She said, "I love you." Her voice was tender and sweet, so unlike the tone she took with Mallory. Mallory's stomach ached with jealousy, but with that came a warm validation; if, past the misery, the woman had found happiness, then maybe Mallory could, too.

The end of the semester loomed. Because her husband would be returning, the woman had said it was time to end things. Mallory frowned, though she'd sensed this was inevitable. Secretly, she hoped they would get together again and thought it best not to betray how devastated she really was.

In mid-December, on what she assumed was their last night together, Mallory took the train into Manhattan to meet the woman for dinner. They went out for sushi, a food Mallory had never eaten before. The restaurant was long and narrow, illuminated only by rectangular lanterns that seemed suspended freely in the air. She ordered what the woman did.

Mallory looked around. She feared the other diners knew they were lovers. Their relationship had only ever occurred within the woman's bedroom, and now it was as if they'd invited others into that room.

The woman asked her what was wrong.

Mallory hesitated. "You're not worried about being recognized?"

The woman thought about this and shrugged. "What do we

even look like?" Then she said, "Are you worried they'll recognize us as having been intimate? Would that make you ashamed?"

To avoid answering right away, Mallory drank some water. There was a slice of lemon wedged on the rim of the glass. She flicked it off and it fell into the drink. With her straw, she pushed the lemon down to the bottom of the glass, past all the ice, and tried to bring it back up. She didn't know how to have a conversation about shame, or even why she felt it.

She said, "It's not you. I'm an only child, right, so I've been used to doing everything alone. And growing up, I don't think I was aware of anyone who, you know, was like me, so I've felt alone in that, too. It just feels like this thing I've had to bear by myself."

The woman stared into her soup bowl. Her despondency, usually kept hidden, blew across the table like a draft. Many of the woman's books were about shame, and Mallory wondered whether the woman's own adolescent shame—over having been born in a country that ignored and was hated for its past, over having lived a normal life while her sister was sick—had dissipated. Mallory wondered whether shame could become so outsized that it went away, like a balloon that swells until it pops.

"Have you always known?" the woman asked Mallory now.

"Probably, yeah. You said you were a miserable child, and I was too, or that's how I remember it. But I think I kind of liked being that way. My next-door neighbor had this dog, Wednesday, named after the daughter from the Addams family, and she thought I resembled her. The character, I mean, not the dog. All broody and dark. I thought that what made me unique was that I was sad. What made me most unhappy was other girls, so I guess I sort of thought that I liked them only because I liked the feeling of being sad."

At this, the woman smiled, which bloomed into a laugh. "Mallory," she said, "I want the world for you."

A waiter arrived with their food and then left. Mallory watched the woman use her chopsticks and then did the same. While Mallory's mouth was full, the woman said, "I understand what you mean. I think that when you're miserable, you often do things that extend that misery. There is something pleasing about misery that makes it seem as though time has stopped."

Mallory swallowed. What the woman said felt true; she felt the woman's words in her own bones, though she didn't know whether this applied to either of them at the moment.

After dinner, they walked through Washington Square Park. Being in Manhattan in December made Mallory imagine she was in a movie. Lights from the enormous Christmas tree in the park twinkled. The park was mostly empty; the few people they saw did not know or care who they were. Despite the cold air she felt warm. She sighed and watched the faint cloud of her breath fade into the night.

The woman brought Mallory underneath the large marble archway marking the square's entrance and kissed her. The kiss was deep and sloppy, as if the woman had become suddenly possessed by a teenager's spirit. After a while, the woman pulled away, and Mallory's mouth swelled from withdrawal. The woman looked wistful, her face filled with the flush of girlhood.

In this moment, Mallory thought she could make out the shape and color of the woman's youth, though she wondered whether that youth had included other girls, another woman.

They hadn't discussed it, and Mallory had been too afraid to ask, worried that doing so would reveal both Mallory's own previous inexperience and what she imagined was the woman's vast romantic background. She didn't want the woman to feel as though she had to take care of her.

Looking around now, knowing the woman had grown up in the city and had gone to college there, Mallory wondered, not yet having any sense of the city's layout, if they were close to Barnard's campus.

"I wish I could have been here with you," Mallory said.

"You would not have wanted to be with me then," said the woman. "I was not a very lovable person."

"I don't think I'm a very lovable person either."

She wanted the woman to tell her she was, to tell her she could be.

But the woman said, "No one is lovable at your age."

Bad People

Mallory's affair with the woman had reminded her of why she loved reading books: to have her own life and innermost feelings reflected back to her. As the next semester started, she began to worry that her own life would not make sense without the woman in it, without the woman mirroring precisely how she—Mallory—felt. Mallory saw her life going forward as inscrutable. It was as if the woman had written her instructions for living in invisible ink.

The woman had said to her once, just after they'd had sex, that Mallory was going to drive someone crazy one day. At the time, Mallory swelled with pride, filled with promise and lust. She had ignored the future tense. After returning to campus following the holiday break, however, she balked at the thought of finding this someone. *No one is lovable at your age.*

She befriended a boy she met in her course on existentialism and phenomenology. In a class of fifteen, she was the only girl. The biweekly lecture was held in a basement. Mallory thought debating the meaning of life in a windowless room full of men was a cruel, if amusing, joke. It was a joke she wanted desperately to share with the woman. But she assumed what the woman wanted most from her at this time was space, so the joke remained an email draft.

The boy's name was Joseph—not Joey or Joe. He was very serious about this, Mallory would learn. He looked just like their professor, who himself was young: the same black hair, the same black scruff, the same thick-framed glasses, the same black jeans cuffed at the ankle. Joseph had an easygoing yet thoughtful attractiveness that Mallory wanted to emulate. She started cuffing her jeans, too.

He saw her doodling one day in the margins of her notebook. She was drawing a portrait of Jean-Paul Sartre based on a photograph from their textbook. They started talking after class, at first about art—he was studying design at the school and worked part-time in the graphics department at a television network in Manhattan. He made images for the channel's college sports shows, despite not having any interest in college sports, or any sports at all. He was a senior and had, he said, a possible full-time job there waiting for him when he graduated.

Mallory asked him, "So you're not going to go backpacking across Europe? Isn't that what people do when they graduate?"

Joseph said, "I don't really care about traveling."

They discussed their favorite movies, their favorite music. She had never told the woman these things; what did the woman care about her music taste?

They read each other's papers on Sartre's "Existentialism Is a Humanism" and debated what it meant that people were condemned to be free. Somehow, this turned into a discussion about sex.

Because Joseph was good-looking, Mallory found flirting with him to be fun. She wondered whether she had ever really flirted with the woman at all.

Joseph ran the indie rock show at the college radio station. Mallory began listening to the show, which aired every night at eight. Sometimes he would dedicate a song to her, pretending she had called in during a commercial break with a request. To hear her name on air gave her a pulse of pleasure. He was working to impress her, and she felt seduced by his effort. Sometimes in bed, if she was alone, she would think of him having sex with her, or even with other girls, and she would touch herself.

❧

He was often invited to concerts for free, and on a Friday night, he invited Mallory to come to one with him. The concert was at a small venue twenty minutes away from campus. He drove them there in his beat-up green Geo. On the way, he drummed his fingers on the steering wheel as they listened to an album that wasn't out yet. The lyrics of a song he played—which seemed to be about having sex in a school library—reminded Mallory of the woman, and she bit her lip to keep from whimpering out of want.

The venue had the sour smell of spilled beer and sweat. Joseph offered to get Mallory a drink, and when he came back, he had only one. He handed it to Mallory, who said, "Where's yours?"

He slipped a finger underneath the wristband the bouncer had put on to show he was of age. The bouncer had fastened it too tight. "I don't drink."

"You don't?"

"My dad was an alcoholic."

"Oh."

"He didn't hit me or my mom or anything. It was more embarrassing than abusive. He couldn't go anywhere without being smashed."

Mallory looked down at her drink. "I'm sorry."

"It's okay. He was a fool. Our lives were fine, right? But he had this horrible childhood, blah blah blah, and I think he wanted his life to not be fine. Some people just crave ruin."

"He's not around anymore?"

"He had this whole other family in Delaware while he was married to my mom. He's with them now."

"Oh my god. Have you met them?"

"Sort of, once. My mom drove me down there to confront him. It was awful. My mom is not usually a dramatic person, and it was like something out of a soap opera. Like, this other woman and her child were just standing on their lawn watching my mom scream at my dad. I remember looking at the other kid, who was a little younger than me, and thinking how weird it was going to be for us to grow up parallel to one another but also totally aware that there was this one moment we shared of seeing our dad as someone different from who we thought he was."

Mallory searched for something to say but could not think of anything right away. She would have normally taken a sip of her drink as a way to buy time, but now it seemed as though the liquid was off-limits. She held the still-full cup by her side.

"A drunk and a bigamist," she finally said. Then she worried joking about it would be crude, so she said, "That must have been hard. It must still be hard."

"It's okay," Joseph said. "I'm over it. What was he going to teach me about being a man?"

"That's a nice way to look at it."

The band Joseph had come to see took the stage. The singer was a girl with bottle-dyed red hair, and she wore lipstick the same garish color. Her voice was startling, like honey filtered through sandpaper. Watching her, mesmerized, Mallory felt her mouth become dry. She looked down at the sticky ground with the sense that a shoelace she kept having to tie had once again slipped loose.

After the show, Joseph drove them to a diner. Waiting to be seated, Mallory became more and more at ease. She was just a girl out and about with a boy. She felt protected by a bubble of normalcy.

They ordered milkshakes, French fries, and a Caesar wrap to split. Mallory asked the waitress if she could bring a side of ranch dressing for the fries. She explained to Joseph that she couldn't stand the taste or smell of ketchup, that it made her feel physically ill. Mallory had never shared this with anyone before. With Joseph, she felt the stakes of intimacy were pleasingly low.

He said, "That's not normal."

She said, "I heard somewhere that if you get sprayed by a skunk, the best thing to do is bathe yourself in ketchup. It's actually so disgusting that it covers up being sprayed by a skunk."

As they ate, Joseph asked her what she thought of the band. Mallory said the singer's voice reminded her of Dolores O'Riordan's from the Cranberries. Joseph said, "Yeah, yeah, that's it." He snarled the word "zombie" like in the song. It surprised her how good this affirmation felt, how glorious it was to come up with the correct point of comparison for two musical acts.

Joseph took a French fry from their plate and dipped it in the ranch dressing. He conceded it was good. Some of the dressing dripped from the fry and onto his beard. He appeared not to notice. Without thinking, Mallory dabbed it with her napkin. The stupid simplicity of this small encounter made her feel content.

B y then, it was the end of February. She had not seen or heard from the woman once in the month since school had resumed. Out of curiosity, she had browsed that semester's course bulletin to see when and where the woman taught. She had class on the opposite side of campus at the same time the woman did, and she knew she would have no real excuse to bump into her.

Mallory wondered whether it was true that absence made the heart grow fonder and when, if ever, the heart became so fond it had to close that absence's gap. Not seeing or hearing from the woman unsettled her; she fretted she had made the whole thing up.

In the last week of February, the university hosted another visiting writer. This writer was someone whose work Mallory loved. She had the writer's collected stories on a shelf in her dorm room and often turned to it for inspiration. She was looking forward to hearing the writer read and maybe meeting her. But she knew the woman would be there too, so she asked Joseph to join her.

The woman was there. She sat in the same seat she always

did. The woman was a creature of habit, Mallory thought, and it was nice to have been that habit. After they'd started seeing each other, they had attended more readings while pretending not to know one another. It had been like a game. Mallory had sat in the back and waited for the woman to find her, and whenever the woman had, Mallory felt as though she was being truly found, like a coin in the sand.

Now, the woman spotted Mallory, glanced at the boy beside her, and then looked back at Mallory. When their eyes met, the woman winced, and they both swallowed. Mallory thought she could feel the woman's spit slide down her own throat. That the woman appeared hurt was, for Mallory, a strange sort of mercy; in this brief look between them, she saw that she had made a mark on the woman's life.

As the visiting writer read from her book, Mallory tried to follow along in her own copy, which she had brought, but the pages appeared impenetrable to her. She had grown up reading these words, had taught herself to write copying these sentences, yet now the paragraphs read like untranslated foreign poetry. Still, she looked only at the book that lay open on her lap. When the writer finished reading and the audience began to clap, Joseph said, louder than Mallory would have liked, "It was adorable watching you follow along."

Afterwards, Mallory met the woman in the restroom.

They were alone. The woman washed her hands and used the mirror to look at Mallory. It was a relief, for Mallory, to see the woman and be seen by her once more, her presence like finding a cool spot on a hot pillow. But the woman glared at her in a way that made her feel as though she'd stuck her head in an oven.

"You've made a new friend," the woman said. "He's handsome."

The woman's apparent anguish aroused Mallory, who became momentarily taken by the drama. "Do you find a lot of students attractive?"

The woman turned and stepped closer to her. She shook water from her hands. The two of them were almost touching now. "Don't do that."

Mallory's heart thumped, and her mouth hung slightly open. Her body braced for the woman's touch.

But the woman stepped backward, as if afraid of what else she might do. She caught sight of the book in Mallory's hand. "Are you a fan? I don't remember hearing you talk about her."

Mallory looked at the book's back cover, the text on its jacket. "I used to copy her sentences into my notebook in high school. They're so strange and sharp. She was my favorite writer's favorite writer."

"Strange and sharp," the woman repeated. "She used to be all the rage."

"You don't like her?"

"She's not for me. When I read her, I can feel her grasping for my attention." Here, the woman snatched at the air in front of her.

This, Mallory understood, was why she found being with the woman so thrilling; it was so easy to fall out of her favor or to bore her that to be the object of her interest, even for a short time, was an accomplishment.

Someone else walked into the bathroom. The woman left, and Mallory followed her, trailing behind her like a child who'd just been scolded in a toy store. "I don't know what to do," Mallory said.

"There's nothing to do," said the woman. She whispered, "We will have to live with what we did."

Mallory was bewildered by what seemed to be an admission of guilt. She felt as though she'd been tossed a live grenade and had no idea what to do with it.

Joseph watched them walk back into the auditorium together, and when Mallory sat down next to him, he said, "Do you know her?"

She took a moment to answer. "Just from coming to these things."

"I know her. Well, I know *of* her." He said the woman's name. Hearing it from someone else was a shock. "I've had friends take her class. I heard she's mean. They call her Eva Braun."

"That is mean," Mallory said, but she offered a little laugh. She did think it was funny, though she felt he was not entirely entitled to the joke.

"You know she writes children's books?"

Mallory said, "I do know that. She illustrates them, too."

He recalled a story in which a friend of his, who'd been interested in pursuing publishing after graduation, had missed the woman's class one time. After the next class, when the girl returned, the woman confronted her and said, "You know, you might need me for a favor one day." Joseph said the woman sounded like a mob boss.

To Mallory, this story sounded true; she could hear the woman say those exact words. Mallory understood the woman, who'd felt helpless all her life, genuinely wanted to help someone else but also wanted that person, whoever they were, to see her as being significant and powerful enough to be of help. Thinking about the woman this way, Mallory swelled with protective affection for her.

Every Saturday morning, Joseph volunteered for an organization called Food Not Bombs, which offered bread and produce that local grocery stores would otherwise discard to people who couldn't afford it. There was a chapter a short drive from the college's campus, and he convinced Mallory to come with him. She would try anything to stop thinking about the woman, though she knew it was no use. *We will have to live with what we did.*

In the winter months, Joseph said, there were fewer volunteers, and when they arrived, they were two of only four people, one of whom had founded this location's group. A small, hungry gathering had already formed, waiting for the food. Mallory and Joseph put two white plastic tables together and arrayed the fruits and vegetables in baskets.

The bread had been baked fresh a day or two earlier, and Mallory, who had not eaten breakfast, found her mouth watering and her stomach rumbling. When, she wondered, was the last time she'd had freshly baked bread? She knew this was a bad thought in that moment and so tried to smile extra widely at the people in line.

"I can't believe you do this," she said to Joseph. "You're such a good person." Then she said, "We have nothing in common."

"There's no such thing as a good man," Joseph said. "Men are incapable of being gallant."

"What do you get out of this?"

"I got you to come out on a date with me, didn't I?"

"Is that what this is? So, it's just about sex then." She pretended to be offended. She took a pear from one of the baskets. "When you see this, you see a shapely woman."

"Yeah, don't you?"

Mallory put the pear back. A man who was in the food line, who had heard this exchange, plucked the pear quickly from its basket and smiled at them.

❦

Mallory's father was going to Florida while she was on spring break. He had been invited by a friend of his to watch Major League Baseball spring training. Feeling that it was pointless to take the train all the way home just to be alone, she stayed on campus. Joy had offered to bring her to Connecticut, but Mallory had her books and the space in which to read them and was looking forward to having the room to herself.

She spent a few days reading and walking around the empty campus. The college had an art gallery, which she browsed with her hands behind her back like a snooty critic. Aside from the receptionist, she was the only person there. She had never really liked—or at least appreciated—museums, which felt so stolid to her, but strolling alone through the gallery, she was moved, remembering that art was something created in hiding that was meant to be found by others.

Before long, though, she became bored.

Joseph, who had also stayed on Long Island, invited Mallory to his house to watch a movie one evening. He lived with his mother, who worked at the college as a secretary, in a house right next to campus. When Mallory entered the house, Joseph's mother was sitting in the living room, watching a rerun of *Friends*. It was the one where no one is ready for Ross's museum benefit. Joseph sat laughing on the arm of the sofa after bringing Mallory inside, and the three of them watched the episode until the credits rolled. Mallory and her own mother had enjoyed this episode, had always laughed when Joey came in wearing all of Chandler's clothes, and now she felt so overcome by her mother's absence that she stood off to the side and said nothing.

They soon ascended a set of stairs and went into Joseph's bedroom. Magazine pages of various musicians and album artwork adorned the walls, some of it signed and personalized. A bass guitar sat in the corner of the room. Mallory plucked the lowest of its strings.

As Mallory fiddled with the instrument, Joseph told her about a *Friends* episode that he had seen as surprisingly profound. It was the one in which Phoebe tries to prove there is such a thing as a selfless act. The only thing she can think of to demonstrate this is allowing a bee to sting her, because how could that benefit her? In the end, the friends tell her it was futile; the bee died after it stung her. Joseph had referenced the episode in a paper for his ethical theory class last semester, comparing it to a part in Plato's *Republic* about a magical ring that grants the wearer the power of invisibility; the man who finds the ring uses it to have an affair with the king's wife, kills the king, and takes over the throne. Even when the ring is given to a man considered just, the result is the same: both a just and unjust person would use it to get what they wanted; how could they resist? The only thing we are capable of doing, Joseph said, is pursuing our own desires. He said this with such earnestness that Mallory didn't know whether to receive it as subtext.

Mallory sat herself down on Joseph's twin-sized bed. They were both quiet for a moment before he found the film they were going to watch on his laptop. It was a movie their existentialism professor had mentioned a few times in class. Despite seeming so young, the professor had just recently gotten divorced, and he told the class that this movie, which starred an aging Bill Murray, had helped him through it. Joseph connected the laptop to his television and joined Mallory on the bed. She moved over to make room.

The movie was slow and sad, and within fifteen minutes, Mallory fell asleep. She woke some time later and saw she had drooled on Joseph's stomach, on which she'd been lying. She looked up at him. He had stayed awake and the movie was almost over. "I'm sorry," she said.

"It's okay," he said. "It's very slow."

Mallory agreed and said, "Misery makes time stop."

"It also loves company."

She picked her head up from his chest. "Are you miserable?"

He laughed softly. "That's not the word I would use. I like my life enough."

She imagined kissing him then—*You can kiss me if you'd like*, she'd say—but she didn't. She imagined a nice, normal life. She imagined being able to tell someone she liked her life enough. But she was who she was.

She got up from the bed, stretched, and sat back down on Joseph's computer chair. On his desk was a copy of *Northanger Abbey*. He was taking a seminar on Jane Austen, which he had enrolled in, he'd told Mallory, to meet girls who were romantically unhappy.

"Can I ask you something?" she said now. "Do I, like, present myself as sad? Is that why you like me?"

"I like you?"

"It's true, right?"

"That makes it sound kind of depressing. I wouldn't say 'sad.' But yeah, I guess. I think I saw you and thought, 'That girl knows.' Does that hurt your feelings? It never comes out right when you try to explain attraction. It's like explaining a joke or a dream."

Mallory thought of why she had first been drawn to the woman and wondered if the woman had been drawn to her for the same reason. She was a sad girl, a lonely girl, and, after a lifetime of practice, she had become so good at this that it had become the most appealing thing about her. This should depress her, she thought, but instead it brought her comfort; at least she was good at something.

⌁

A week later, the campus came back to life. Having been alone at the college made Mallory covet it, and her fellow students appeared to her now as trespassers.

One afternoon in mid-March, Joseph didn't show up to class. Before the lecture began, Mallory texted him to ask where he was. All he said in response was, *Come hang out after?*

She looked around at the other students, whom she hadn't really taken stock of before. She wondered whether they were good people. They were mostly blurry for her; she could not imagine what their real lives were like outside of discussing Nietzsche. Watching them, she worried she lacked empathy. Their lives seemed as small as, if not smaller than, her own.

Mallory followed along with the lecture, which was on *Twilight of the Idols*. She chewed on her pen, taking it out of her mouth on occasion to underline the aphorisms she thought spoke to her own life: "The perfect woman indulges in literature just as she indulges in a small sin; as an experiment, in passing, looking around to see if anybody notices it—and to make sure that someone does."

After class, she walked to Joseph's house. Instead of ringing the doorbell, she texted him that she was there. Yet when the door opened, it was Joseph's mother on the other side.

His mother beamed. "Mallory," she said. "It's so nice of you to stop by."

Their first meeting had been tempered by the television, but now Mallory felt confronted with the fact of Joseph's mother, and her face flushed. She worried her motherlessness, which Joseph knew about and had maybe relayed, was stamped across her forehead.

"Is everything okay?" Mallory asked.

"He's not feeling well. But I'm sure he'll be happy to see you."

"That's okay, I'll go."

"Don't worry, it's not contagious." She stepped aside to allow Mallory in the house. "It's just food poisoning. The worst of it is over."

To leave now, Mallory thought, would be rude. She felt duped.

Upstairs, Joseph was lying propped up in bed. His eyes were closed, and he wore large headphones over his ears. He looked pale; his tanned complexion—his father's family was Mediterranean, from Sicily, he'd said—was blanched of its usual color. A plastic bucket sat beside his bed.

Mallory remained in the doorframe. Joseph's mouth was lolled open in a way that reminded her of her mother on morphine, drool pooling on her lip before dropping onto her hospital gown. Mallory had the growing sense that Joseph wanted something from her that she was unable to give; both his asking and her lacking irked her. Any initial sympathy she experienced for him dissolved into an annoyance so red-hot it made her sweat.

She rapped her knuckle on the wall beside the door to let him know she was there.

He opened his eyes and smiled, taking off his headphones. "You're here. How was class?"

"It was fine. Why did you want me to come over if you were like this?"

"I wanted to see you."

"Like this? Why?"

He gestured toward his computer chair. "You can sit if you want. I won't hurl on you."

Mallory took a step into the room but didn't sit. "I have a lot of work to do. Just tell me when you're better."

"Really, I'm fine. I went out for dinner with a guy from work.

I had this cheeseburger with guacamole on top. The whole night was awful."

He started to tell a story about another coworker of his who had, earlier that evening, before he got sick, wronged him in a small way that to him felt catastrophic. Mallory did not know or care about this person. It was a pleasant day outside, still chilly but the sun shone bright. As he spoke, she became aware of how little daylight there was left. His story filled her ears the way music from a radio punctures a peaceful reverie on the beach. She couldn't wait to be back in her room, alone with her own thoughts.

"Why are you telling me this?" she asked him. "And why right now?"

Her insolence struck him dumb. "Do you not care about my life?"

"This seems so inconsequential."

"It was annoying."

"I'm sorry, but so is hearing about it."

"This is what people do. If we didn't talk about the inconsequential things that annoyed us, no one would talk about anything."

"But it's like hearing about a dream. No one wants to hear about that. That's the best part of having dreams. They're insane and they only make sense to you."

"I'm not sure what's happening right now."

"I'm going to go," she said, turning to leave. But then she turned back. "I hope you feel better."

It took a long time for her irritation to die down, and as she walked back to her dorm room, she experienced the onset of a migraine. Her head felt as though it was filled past capacity. Her vision was cloudy, darkness encroaching from the corners. The muscles in her neck knotted. Her migraines had begun when she was ten, the year her mother first became sick, and she had gotten them often the last year of her mother's life. Realizing this, Mallory imagined her body as having its own consciousness separate from the rest of her, and that the headaches were her body's way of putting her focus back on her own problems. Medically, she thought, this could be true—who knew? The body does what it wants.

When she arrived back at her room, there was maybe an hour of daylight left, but she thought of that hour as hers.

She knew that Joseph would be upset with her, and he was. They didn't speak at all when he returned to class, and after the lecture, they went their separate ways. It was the first time in a long time, Mallory thought, that she had hurt someone. She didn't know how to feel about this. That she had the ability to wound meant she was important, but this importance came with a responsibility that discomfited her.

She walked across the campus to where the woman's office was. The woman was inside.

Mallory knocked.

The woman, who did not look surprised to see her, waved her in. She told Mallory to close the door.

Mallory wanted to run and throw herself at the woman's feet. Instead, she flumped herself down on the blue plastic chair next to the woman's desk. The chair was uncomfortable, and she thought of what the woman had said about no one ever visiting her. Once, as a joke, Mallory had declared that she was going to take the woman's class; gravely, however, the woman forbade her: "It wouldn't be right."

Still, sitting in the woman's office now, Mallory felt she was in the right place. It was bright outside but had started drizzling; by visiting the woman, she'd narrowly escaped getting wet.

The woman had taken out a stack of papers to grade, and a part of Mallory felt comforted that the woman wanted nothing from her.

"Thank you for not making a scene a few weeks ago," the woman said.

"I wouldn't do that."

"I know."

"I'm not going to tell anyone."

"I know that, too." The woman sat in silence. She flipped the page on a student's paper. In the margin, she drew a check with her red pen. "I felt a little jealous."

"You did?"

"Wasn't that your intention?"

Mallory gave a shaky laugh and shrugged.

"Do you not think I care about you?" the woman asked. "I think about you all the time."

"I think about you all the time, too."

The woman scanned another page, then another. The paper was finished, and the woman gave it an A. "What is that saying about how when you get a chill it's because someone has walked over your grave? Sometimes it seems like I can sense when you're thinking of me."

Mallory said, "It's hard to know how you feel about me."

The woman looked at her then. "Listen," the woman whispered, which made Mallory worry she herself had been talking too loudly. "You and I understand one another in a way that, you will learn, is very rare. These last few months have not been easy for me. I've missed the way you look at me."

Mallory looked up at the woman, feeling how wide her own eyes were, wanting to take in whatever the woman wanted to offer. She imagined she watched the woman the way a child looks at someone who is reading her a book.

"Yes," the woman said, "like that. You have to know how good that feels. You have to know how horrible it is not to have it."

It was easy for Mallory to view the woman this way. With other people, she often felt she had to feign interest in what they were talking about, rearranging her face so she appeared eager to receive their boring stories. She suspected other people knew this about her, her wild struggle to show interest in them; she was, despite an entire adolescence spent in hiding, a bad liar. This was not how it was with the woman. Everything the woman said seemed worth writing down to remember. Every story the woman told and gesture she made felt to Mallory as if it was unlocking another latch to the door to her own life. When she thought about the woman, she thought thrillingly about her own self and what she could be.

Mallory held her head in her hand in such a way that her wrist, which the woman often kissed, was on display. She said, "You can have it whenever you want."

꙳

The next day, there was an email from the woman inviting Mallory to her house. She gave a specific time and said, *I'll only be available for a couple of hours.*

When Mallory arrived at the woman's house, there were

store-bought cookies on the counter. They had white chocolate chunks and macadamia nuts. Mallory leaned over the counter in a pose she hoped was suggestive and flicked her finger on the cookie container's plastic lid. She sauntered over to the woman and they kissed, as they often had, standing there in the kitchen. Upon pulling away, the woman whispered in Mallory's ear, "It's good you don't wear perfume."

Mallory thought this meant the woman liked how she smelled, and it was only later, after they had sex, which had occurred on top of the covers in the guest room, that she realized the woman was worried she'd leave behind her scent.

The guest room was much smaller than the main bedroom. It was sparsely decorated, the air stuffy and stale. It was on the side of the house that faced the street, and Mallory could hear the shadowy gauze of the passing cars.

Sitting up in bed, the woman began removing nail polish from her fingers using tiny cotton balls. As she did this, she said, "A few years ago, we repainted our living room. We had to re-move a framed painting that received a lot of compliments when people came over, but once the living room was done, the paint-ing no longer looked good where it used to be, so we put it away and forgot to take it back out. That's what being married for a long time is like."

"Where's the painting now?"

"It's still in storage," the woman said. "For a while, I had almost forgotten about it. But some months later, after we finished redoing the room, a friend came over and said, 'Hey, whatever happened to that painting?' I realized I missed it." She smiled and patted Mallory on the head.

The woman got up from the bed. She cracked open a window, which felt like a reprieve, and asked Mallory to get dressed. Then she asked Mallory to repaint the nails on her right hand. Mallory laughed, but the woman was serious. "You're an artist," she said. "And it will obscure the smell."

They sat at the kitchen counter. The woman told Mallory to watch as she put the new paint, an eggplant purple, on her left hand. As Mallory watched, she thought of her mother, whose nail-biting habit had been so bad at the end of her life that she'd had to apply a bad-tasting chemical lacquer on them to prevent herself from putting them in her mouth.

After Mallory was done with the woman's right hand, the woman offered her a cookie. Mallory ate it as the woman's fingers dried.

"Why are you wasting your time with that boy?" said the woman. "You should date someone like you. A girl, I mean."

"Did you date girls when you were younger?"

The woman glanced down at her hands on the table. She spread her fingers farther apart from one another. "I have slept with other women, yes. But I'm not like you. We are alike in many ways, but not that one."

"Which ways are we alike?"

The woman looked as if she knew Mallory was going to ask this. "You and I," she said, "we do what we do in the dark and then we deal with it all alone." She puckered her lips and blew onto her nails. "That's how I know you won't tell anyone about us. If you did, whatever this is would no longer be just yours."

They met infrequently. Weeks went by without them seeing one another. Whenever they were together, the woman was in a rush and sometimes seemed upset, even though it was the woman who always determined when they met. To pass the time in between their meetings, Mallory masturbated; this meant when they did have sex, she often took a long time to come. If she took longer than usual, she would feel as though she was wasting the woman's time, so she'd fake it.

For the most part, Mallory liked to imagine it was the woman's husband causing the woman's distress, as if he was a thorn in her side only Mallory could remove.

A student on his Rate My Professors page had identified him as a "silver fox." Next to his name was a red tamale, which meant someone had found him hot. She looked hard at his author photo, wanting to see him the way the woman did, wanting to see the kind of person the woman had made a life with. Mallory found where his office was, where he taught. She thought she could plausibly engage him in conversation about his book or could even solicit his advice on stocks. She wanted to dislike him strongly but imagined that the woman was a difficult person to love.

On the phone with her father one day, Mallory asked what it was like to be married. He said, "Why, have you met someone? Whoever he is, it seems a little soon for marriage." She told him no. He was quiet. Then he said marriage was like the card game War: the pain and pleasure of it came from how long it lasted. After he said this, he became giddy, as if proud of his cleverness. He gathered a notebook—"Hold on," he said—to scratch it down. Days are filled with small-scale squabbles, he said. Sometimes you win, sometimes you don't. But you just keep playing. To Mallory, this seemed exhausting.

"I'm glad we're talking about this," he said.

"You are?"

He paused. He had met someone, he said. She was a widow and lived most of the year in Argentina. She had family in America whom she visited every few months. They'd been set up by mutual friends. Listening to him describe the widow, Mallory thought she understood her father's desire for a relationship with those geographical and emotional parameters.

When she got off the phone, she wobbled back and forth between gratitude and resentment. Her father had kept the severity of her mother's final illness from her; while she was thankful that she hadn't had to confront it squarely, she still begrudged him keeping it a secret. This had given him a lot of power over her, making her feel, when her mother did die, like an idiot.

The next time she saw the woman, she relayed her father's marriage analogy to her. She sat at the woman's kitchen counter and spun softly on the stool. The woman watched Mallory struggle to sit still. Mallory felt the heat of her gaze. To stop herself from spinning, she lifted her leg and rested it on the counter. The woman looked at Mallory. "Could you not sit like that?"

"Sorry."

"To help sit up straight, cross your legs at the calf."

"Okay," Mallory said. She did just that.

"Marriage like War," the woman said. "That's good."

"It doesn't sound good."

"Relationships are hard. Often they're not worth it."

"How can you say that?"

"From experience. I have been with my husband for a long time. When I met him, I thought, 'This is okay.' Sometimes it's not okay. There have been whole years of our marriage when I thought, 'What is going on? Why are we doing this?'"

Mallory repeated the questions back to her: "What is going on? Why are we doing this?" She did this not because she wanted the woman to answer them but because their silliness and simplicity surprised her. *What is going on? Why are we doing this?* These didn't seem like questions to ask about something as significant as a marriage.

The woman must have thought Mallory wanted the questions answered, or that Mallory was mocking her. She narrowed her eyes. A laugh broke through, curious and brusque. Any levity the laugh produced soon dissolved. Mallory had overplayed a hand she hadn't even been dealt.

"Don't make light of something you don't understand," the woman said.

"You mean marriage?"

"You're young," the woman said, pushing herself away from the counter. "Go be young. I need to take care of some grown-up things." She slapped a twenty-dollar bill on the countertop, called Mallory a taxi, and walked into her office.

❦

Weeks passed. By then, the school year was nearly over, and summer break was coming soon. Mallory began to worry she would never see the woman again. She reloaded her email with diminishing hope. She thought about nothing else but how terrible she felt; there was nothing else beyond it. But there was also a pleasing insularity to her sorrow. There was something about misery that made it seem as though time had stopped.

Wallowing in her heartache, Mallory sat for long spells in the college's arboretum. The once-denuded trees slouched with the weight of new leaves. She listened to some of the mixtapes Joseph had made for her, and to Carole King's *Tapestry*. "It's Too Late" had been her mother's favorite song. It was a love song, but every time she heard it now, she imagined singing the words to her mother. *Now you look so unhappy, and I feel like a fool.*

Listening to the music Joseph had given her made Mallory miss him. In just a few weeks, he might leave her life forever too, since he was a senior and would graduate. She was surprised by how much this saddened her.

She approached him after class one day and apologized. He said it was fine, that she was clearly going through something. Mallory said, "Yeah, I guess."

The following Saturday, she went with him to help hand out food to the homeless, and afterwards he drove them to Heckscher

State Park. There, they sat along the shoreline. The day was overcast, in the low sixties. The sea-salt wind swept over them, and they huddled close together to stay warm.

He'd brought two sandwiches from a deli near campus and handed her one. Mallory laughed and said, "You're full of charity today."

"You're needy in a different way," he said.

"In what way am I needy?"

He looked at her side-eyed. "In the way that you want something but don't know what it is."

Mallory watched the waves. "I know what it is."

The sandwiches were wrapped in waxed paper, which snapped in the wind as they unfastened it. They used a pair of Frisbees he had in his car as plates.

"I could introduce you to someone," Joseph said. "I know a lot of girls."

She took a bite of her sandwich and chewed. She swallowed. "Okay."

"I have a type, I guess. The first time a girl broke up with me for another girl, I felt very emasculated, you know? The second time, I was like, 'Oh, I get it, it's because I'm *too much* of a man.'"

Mallory laughed. She was glad he made a joke out of it.

"I thought you were going to kiss me," he said. "That night we watched the movie. When you didn't, I was like, 'I see what's going on here.'"

"Because who could resist you?"

He held out his hands.

"You would have kissed me back?" Mallory asked.

"I'm not a saint."

After they ate, they threw one of the Frisbees back and forth. At first, she was terrible at it. She almost tossed the disc into the water. He taught her how to flick her wrist, though, and soon she was watching the Frisbee sail freely through the air. She glanced frequently at the ocean with the feeling that there was a lot of life before her.

⌇

Just before Mallory left for summer break, the woman emailed her. They arranged to meet at her house later that same day. To make their meeting, Mallory had to skip a study session with some other students from her class.

When Mallory arrived, the woman came to the door. Mallory glanced up at her, feeling both jubilant and glum.

"You came," the woman said. Her lips were stained dark with wine. Opening the door wider, she pulled Mallory inside and said, "What a terrible week."

Sober, Mallory found the woman's drunkenness bothersome. She was unsure of what to do or say, and in this uncertainty she did and said nothing. She took her shoes off and left them by the door.

Once she was inside, the woman gave her a kiss. The kiss was harsh and wet. When she pulled away, she asked, "How are you?"

"Fine," said Mallory.

The woman smiled widely. "No one ever means that." She took Mallory's hand and kissed her wrist.

Mallory wondered whether the woman was deliberately ignoring their last encounter. Maybe, she thought, the woman's drunkenness was meant to compensate for it. "I'm sorry," Mallory said, "for the last time I was here."

Elation fell from the woman's face. "Sorry, sorry," she sneered. "You don't have to apologize."

To stop herself from apologizing for her apology, she asked the woman if she had any plans for the summer. The woman was going to Hiddensee, an island off the coast of Germany. What the woman said was, "We're going to Hiddensee," and for a moment, Mallory thought she meant the two of them.

"I want your life," Mallory said.

"I'm sure you'll have it someday."

The woman walked into the kitchen to get a glass of water. Mallory was struck dumb by the portent of the woman's words. She stood still in the foyer. She didn't think the woman wanted to be followed, so instead she walked past the dining area and into the living room. She stood in front of the large window overlooking the pool, which had a tarp covering it since the weather was still too cold for a swim. Her body reflected in the glass appeared vague, a sketch that hadn't yet been filled in.

The two of them sat on the sofa and stared at the turned-off television. They kissed some more, but the woman's intoxication had turned into tiredness. Mallory inched closer to the woman, wanting to feel the warmth of her body. Being touched by the woman had so often felt like putting pressure on a wound.

After a flicker of hesitation or surprise, the woman lifted her arm to accept Mallory's embrace. Mallory rested her head on the woman's shoulder and wrote her own name with her fingernail on the woman's leg. What she wrote was her signature, which she had been practicing since she was a child in case she became famous. Over and over Mallory signed her name on the woman's leg before erasing it with her palm.

The woman looked up at the ceiling. Instinctively, Mallory did the same. The woman asked, "Are we bad people?" She said this with an odd, childlike lilt, which was off-putting and made Mallory bristle.

Mallory thought of how, many months earlier, the woman had told her a story about having lunch with an old friend, someone the woman considered a genuinely good person, and how, conceitedly, the woman had felt she was terrible in contrast. Mallory and the woman had laughed together about this, their insensitivity a devious secret. Mallory loved thinking of the woman as selfish because she felt it granted herself permission to be selfish; the woman's willingness to behave badly, even in middle age, absolved Mallory of a lot of guilt. Now, the woman's drunken remorse made Mallory feel as though she needed to protect this person—this woman—from something. She didn't know how to take care of the woman. She knew only how to take care of herself.

I Love That I Can
Tell You Things

Growing up, Mallory had heard her mother referred to as "the pretty sister," while her aunt was "the funny one." When she herself was very young, Mallory sometimes imagined she had a twin sister who had died in the womb. The sister would have been the pretty one.

Mallory's aunt, the funny one, died of ovarian cancer when Mallory was eight. At the end of her life, she was in hospice care at home, and the day she died, the family sat in a crescent around her bed. Mallory was unsettled by the jaundiced yellow of her aunt's skin. She used to tell Mallory dirty jokes when no one else was in earshot—*Have I told you the one about the man who died from a Viagra overdose? They couldn't close the casket*—and now she was gone.

Two years after her aunt died, her mother got breast cancer. (Throughout her childhood, Mallory thought the phrase "spreading like cancer" meant cancer was contagious, like a cold.) Her mother sat her down on the living-room floor and explained that she had a lump in her breast and that she would eventually lose all her hair. They spent the next hour lying on the floor together, flipping through a picture book that illustrated John Lennon's "Imagine" in pastel colors.

Her mother had a double mastectomy and had to replace her breasts with balloons. The image of a balloon was pleasing to Mallory, almost celebratory, but her mother worried aloud that she had lost a part of herself. She had been the pretty one.

The balloons were pads made of silicone, and shortly after the procedure when they were put in, one of them began leaking; "deflated" was the word Mallory's father used. For Mallory, who'd been born with a lazy eye and later developed a cyst on one of her ovaries, this meant that her mother was lopsided too. If the two of them were halves, then together they could make a whole.

Because she saw herself as a girl only a mother could love, she often wanted to be alone, but if she couldn't be alone, then she wanted to be the center of attention, which felt like a way to exert control over her aloneness. Throughout grade school, she was the class clown. She repeated things to her classmates that her aunt had said. *When the pirate asked me where my buccaneers were, I told him they were under my buckin' hat.* The other kids laughed. If she couldn't be pretty, then at least she could be funny.

☙

Like Mallory, Hannah Allard was an only child. They met when Hannah and her family moved into the house next door. Hannah was a year older—eleven to Mallory's ten. This was just after Mallory's mother started chemotherapy. When Mallory learned a family with a daughter her age was moving in next door, she became hopeful that her life would change, that she would be granted access to the parts of the world only available to girls who had friends.

The day Hannah arrived, Mallory watched from her parents' bedroom window, which overlooked the Allards' driveway. Mrs. Allard, Hannah's mother, drove a Jeep Grand Cherokee. Hannah stumbled out of the Jeep looking plump and slumberous, almost like a human-sized version of the bedrest pillow Mallory's mother referred to as a "husband." But Hannah had a latent beauty about her, more feminine anyway than Mallory, and watching her, Mallory thought, *You can be the pretty one.*

Hannah was carrying a book, the title of which Mallory strained to see but couldn't. She went into her bedroom to see if there was a book on her own shelf that she would be willing to swap with Hannah; to exchange stories with another girl had been a daydream of hers, though the fantasy had been to have other people read what Mallory told them to read, so that they would understand her more without her having to explicitly tell them. Mallory's mother, however, had often said never to lend a book unless you didn't want to see it again. She looked through her comic collection and got so caught up reading some of the issues that she eventually forgot about Hannah.

It was a mild afternoon in mid-July. Mallory's father had shut off the air-conditioning and opened all the doors and windows. Mallory didn't mind this, since air-conditioning made her skin prickle. Her mother was sitting outside on the screened-in porch reading Audre Lorde's *Cancer Journals*.

The quiet that had settled over the house was punctured by Hannah's voice shouting, "Wednesday!"

Mallory went outside to join her mother on the porch and followed her mother's gaze to a spot in the backyard where a big, black dog was rummaging through Mallory's old sandbox. The dog's sleek fur was strikingly dark against the bright day.

It was then that Hannah and her mother came over. The two of them had the same face, glowing and round, like moons. Mallory's mother was wearing a wig, and the last thing she wanted, Mallory knew, was to meet someone new.

Mallory pointed to the sandbox. "Wednesday?"

"We're so sorry," Mrs. Allard said. "And you were just out here reading. A woman after my own heart."

"It's no trouble," Mallory's mother said. She closed her book, hiding its jacket, and fingered the ends of her fake hair.

"I like to read, too," said Mallory.

Mrs. Allard smiled at her.

Hannah ran to the dog, squatted, and held Wednesday in her arms. For a moment, Mallory imagined herself as the dog, how good that kind of devotion would feel from a girl her age. She left the porch and walked toward them. She heard her mother offer Hannah a glass of water, but Mrs. Allard asked, "Anything stronger?" Mallory listened to the two of them snicker, wanting to be let in on the joke, caught between making a new friend and sitting with the adults while they sipped their conspiratorial white wine.

The dog continued to sniff around the sandbox. Up close, Wednesday's eyes looked both inquisitive and sad. "I think he wants something that's in there," Hannah said.

Mallory thought she knew what the dog was after but said nothing.

"Do you have a dog?" Hannah asked.

"I had a hamster," Mallory said, "but it died from pinkeye. He's buried under the sandbox. I think that's what Wednesday wants." She felt a little embarrassed, as if the slight shame she felt over this—that she hadn't been able to take care of such a simple pet, that it had died in this ludicrous way—had been made tangible, taken from her, and shown back to her.

Hannah looked at her askance but then laughed. "Don't you get pinkeye from farting on a pillow? I didn't know you could die from that." She picked up a stick and waved it in front of Wednesday's face before throwing it a few feet away. Wednesday chased after it and brought it back. "He likes to run away," Hannah said of Wednesday, "but he never makes it very far. My mom says he likes the idea of escape but not the reality of it."

❧

Almost every day that summer, they sat outside on Hannah's deck while Hannah's father and uncle built a wooden fence so Wednesday couldn't flee. It was always Hannah's house, never Mallory's, and this was the latter's choice; at Hannah's, Mallory could escape the oppressive worries of her mother's illness. She and Hannah chewed carelessly on celery stalks slicked with chunky peanut butter and drank whole pitchers of iced tea brewed by Mrs. Allard. Hannah's mother had a large collection of art books, and Mallory and Hannah—both of whom wanted to be artists when they grew up—would compete to see who could better copy famous paintings freehand. Mallory wanted to win, if only to impress Mrs. Allard, whom she could sense floating around them.

They also liked to read each other the sex advice from women's magazines, rubbing Banana Boat tanning oil on their skin and spouting the tips and tricks aloud. They spoke quietly, with hot scoffs, though speaking in this clandestine way was thrilling.

One afternoon in August, Mallory accompanied her mother to the local pharmacy, planning to shoplift a *Cosmopolitan* for Hannah while her mother picked up her prescriptions.

The pharmacy was small, made up of a half dozen narrow aisles. Security cameras were trained only on the entrance and the register; the magazines were shelved in a blind spot along with a couple of popular paperbacks. While her mother filled her prescriptions, Mallory slid the *Cosmo* into the front of her pants. To keep it from moving around, she had to lodge it inside her underwear.

When the magazine was secure, Mallory joined her mother at the register. The pharmacist was the grandfather of one of her classmates and she smiled at him warmly. Her amiable acknowledgement of him and the sad specificity of the medications her mother was receiving—Zofran for nausea, Ativan for anxiety—immunized her, she thought, from any suspicion on the pharmacist's part.

She asked her mother if she could buy a pack of Hot Tamales. These too were for Hannah; they were, Mallory had learned, Hannah's favorite candy. Mallory's mother paid in cash and placed the coins from her change into a cup marked with the logo of a children's cancer fund. Her mother looked at the cup and said, "Sometimes the world makes it so hard to feel sorry for yourself."

They left the pharmacy, but on the way to the car, her mother stopped to root around in her purse for her keys. It was a large purse, absurdly so, and she often lost things inside it. Impatient, Mallory kept walking to the car, which was parked toward the back of the small lot. Two spaces away, in the very last spot, a man sat in his car and masturbated.

At ten years old, Mallory didn't totally know what the man was doing, though she knew it was considered vulgar. This made the sight of him all the more thrilling. His windows were closed shut, but the loud breath of the air conditioner, turned all the way up, perhaps to drown out the sound of his grunts, wafted from the car. On his lap was an open magazine with a naked woman taking up the whole page. His head was thrown back against the headrest in a way that looked religious. Mallory became newly aware of the *Cosmo* pressed into her pelvis. She felt a fresh slickness against the magazine's gloss.

Her mother didn't notice the man, and as they drove back home Mallory carried the mental picture of him jerking off like she'd pocketed a shiny rock. She carried it across the yard to Hannah's house.

Hannah's glee over the candy and the *Cosmo* softened Mallory's unease over the magazine's slightly wrinkled dampness and sour smell. It was just after noon, but Hannah was still wearing her nightclothes: a big, blue Buffalo Bills T-shirt with O. J. Simpson's name and number emblazoned on the back. Hannah's family had moved to New Jersey from Buffalo; it had been her father's shirt. After O. J.'s acquittal, her father had wanted to burn it, but Hannah, who was seven at the time of the trial, began wearing it to bed instead. She also, Mallory knew, kept a cache of the crime-scene photos on the family computer in a folder marked "Boring Homework."

They spent the afternoon lazing as they usually did on Hannah's back porch. Hannah's father and uncle were almost done building the fence for Wednesday. *Cosmo* called for them to drip melted ice onto their lovers' bodies. It also suggested you put your hand on your man's heart so you could feel how wild you were driving him.

As she read, Mallory thought of the man in the car and his cramped desire. Instead of being put off, she felt a perverse joy; before that day, the only penis she'd seen was a crude drawing in a public toilet. She knew Hannah had never seen one, either. That she became privy to something before Hannah, who was a year older, made her think she would be more successful later in life.

"Tell me something else," Hannah said. Often Mallory looked for strange facts on the internet or under the tops of Snapple bottles in order to relay them to Hannah later. Appearing knowledgeable about interesting things made her feel as though she was invaluable.

Mallory said, "Did you know the tongue is the strongest muscle in the human body?"

Hannah stuck out her tongue. "What else?"

"You can't tickle yourself."

Hannah began fiddling with her armpit. When she found it didn't do anything, she tried to tickle Mallory, who squirmed and told her to stop.

Mallory said, "Did you know that lips are red because they have a lot of blood in them?" She puckered her lips in anticipation of a kiss. Hannah, however, reached a finger toward Mallory's mouth and flicked her lips.

After they'd had enough sun, the two of them went swimming. The Allards had inherited an aboveground pool from the house's previous owners, though it was built high up underneath a large tree and did not receive much of the sun's light.

In the pool, they sank themselves below the surface and watched each other swim. The water was cold, and to get warm, they took turns snaking their way around one another, coiling their legs around each other's waists. Mallory thought that if she could breathe, she would have stayed underwater with Hannah forever. Below the surface, there was nothing and no one else. There was no other sound but the whoosh and warble of the aquatic world.

⌄

When Hannah was in seventh grade and Mallory in sixth, they discovered that three brothers on their block grew their own pot. The youngest of them was Hannah's age, and when Hannah found out they were selling it, she suggested she and Mallory try it. They knew other kids at school who did drugs, even harder ones, and did not want to feel left out. Despite this, however, they were terrified of smoking with others who had already done it, worried they would be teased for their inexperience. This was, Mallory understood, the pleasure of a close, hermetical friendship, the freedom of remove.

The first time, they purchased a gram from the youngest brother for ten dollars—a neighborhood discount, the boy said— and after school, they brought the little bag to the woods at the end of their block. Hannah took a can of Cherry Coke from her backpack, drank most of it in one gulp, and emptied the rest onto the ground. In the dirt, the soda fizzed and settled. Its glisten made Mallory a little forlorn, as if the discarded liquid was itself upset about being poured out. Hannah then sat on the empty can, crushing it with her ass. With a pen, she poked a hole in the middle of the can and sprinkled the weed on top, lighting it and sucking out the smoke from the can's mouth. She'd researched how to do this on the internet.

Feeling as if her first hit didn't do anything, Hannah pulled from her pocket a piece of folded-up notebook paper. In addition to looking up how to make a bong from a soda can, she had researched how to properly inhale. She'd been a straight-A student all her life.

"The best thing about the internet," Hannah said, "is that you're never alone. There's always some dweeb who couldn't do what you can't do and somehow figured it out." She referred to her notes as she tried another hit. This time seemed to please her, and she nodded as if she'd discovered something very valuable about life. When she passed the can to Mallory, she said, "You can even learn how to kiss."

Mallory, also not knowing how to inhale, tried inconspicuously to read Hannah's notes upside down. But thinking about kissing made Hannah's handwriting hard for her to focus on. She pictured the two of them taking turns kissing a dummy, like a target used for archery. Then she pictured them kissing each other. Hannah saw that Mallory was having difficulty reading the notes so repositioned them for a better view. Mallory followed the steps and, glancing at Hannah's lips, began to cough.

"That's good," Hannah said. "They said it's good when you cough."

"It hurts," said Mallory.

"Maybe it's like exercising. You know how people say, 'No pain, no gain?'" Hannah held a hand on her belly. "Take it from me; I'm an expert."

Mallory laughed, which made her throat hurt more.

When the little bit of weed was finished, they sat for a while, quiet, with their backs against a cluster of bamboo stalks, which had always felt random and exotic to them in the woods near their neighborhood, so wildly out of place. Mallory's mouth was dry. She licked her lips but became increasingly worried when they didn't seem to get wet. Over and over she stuck out her tongue and swept it across her mouth until Hannah started to laugh and told her to relax. Hannah's gentle gibe put Mallory at ease. She was glad they'd done this alone together.

Before they left the woods, Hannah sprayed them both down with a fruity mist. Hungry, they trundled back to Hannah's house, but on the way, they saw the dealer and his brothers in their driveway playing basketball with some friends. It was shirts versus skins. The dealer's upper body was scrawny and bare. Hannah stood and stared. Mallory watched Hannah watch the boys play their game, understanding that she should be stirred by the sight of them too and frustrated that she was not. As the boys looked back at the two of them, she felt the sudden swell of a curtain being pulled open and that she was alone on a stage. She tugged on Hannah's arm. "Let's go," she said. "I'm starving. I'll die if I don't eat."

When they got back to Hannah's house, Hannah opened a big

bag of potato chips but didn't eat any. Mallory couldn't help herself and ate half the bag.

⌁

By the end of seventh grade, Hannah started to obsess over losing weight. Pot made her hungry, so she stopped smoking it. She replaced weed with an occasional cigarette, which curbed her appetite, and which she smoked in secret; only Mallory knew.

By eighth grade, she became bulimic. Puking up her food allowed her to shed the shell of childhood. Protruding cheekbones reduced her face's roundness, and the kinks in her tawny hair unfurled into brownish-blond tufts that caught light like kindling. She was, more than ever, the pretty one.

Whenever they went to the mall now, Hannah would be catcalled. Once, after Mallory had stolen a Yankee Candle from the Hallmark Store—the candle was scented like a McIntosh apple, Hannah's favorite smell—a man rushed up from behind the two of them. Mallory thought it was a Hallmark employee and panicked, but it was just some guy. He grinned at Hannah and said, "I had to see if the front looked as good as the back."

It was the first time either of them had been the object of obvious predation. Past the immediate fear of being followed and raped, Mallory felt jealous. That she was not subjected to something heinous meant that she was so unremarkably unpretty as to not even be preyed upon. Hannah gave a nervous laugh, while Mallory looked for the nearest exit. Neither of them knew what time it was, and whether Hannah's mother was waiting for them in the car; Mallory imagined them being chased but narrowly escaping in Mrs. Allard's Jeep. Instead, they walked into Old Navy, where the man didn't follow them.

"Oh my god," Mallory said.

"I know," said Hannah. She looked down at her chest and adjusted her breasts. "Do you think he was disappointed?"

❧

For a while, Mallory smoked pot by herself. She read about how to roll joints from the internet; it was true what Hannah had said about learning anything online. Also, she became obsessively interested in horror films. It started with *The Thing*, a movie that was, to Mallory, about being a really good liar. At first, she made Hannah watch these movies with her, wanting to share the experience of being scared, but Hannah didn't care for them. It was just as well, Mallory felt; vanishing alone, while high, into a two-hour nightmare became almost as sacred as prayer. She liked having something of her own.

Eventually, however, smoking pot by herself felt dull, and also became expensive, so instead, when she got to high school, she sold it.

Hannah had stayed in the public-school system, but Mallory's parents sent her to a private school, one that had offered her a partial art scholarship. She found the rich kids there paid twice as much for weed, so she bought eighths for thirty-five dollars from the boy down the street and sold them in separate pieces for twenty dollars each. Despite the smallness of the quantity, this made her a fair amount of money.

Hannah did not like Mallory selling pot. She thought it was

silly and said, "Who does that?" She called Mallory "Scarface." Mallory, however, relished the invisible significance afforded to her as a small-time weed dealer. At her school, boys and girls who otherwise ignored her sought her out. Many of her classmates knew who she was without her having to make an effort to know them.

Mallory became taken with this idea of partial self-isolation. She wore mostly black clothes to school, and when she wasn't in class, she had her earbuds in, listening to scores from horror films. She sat by herself at lunch and read novels by Stephen King or Dean Koontz, and after classes ended each day, she went to the school's art studio, which was in the basement of a building tucked away toward the back end of the campus, where she worked for long, uninterrupted hours on whatever she wanted. She even taught herself how to throw pottery.

Since the studio was in a basement, the small windows, like portholes, showed only the other students' feet. She'd watch them walk by. Once, she saw two pairs of feet stop in front of the window; a boy in loafers leaned back against the side of the building while a girl in Birkenstocks stood on her toes to kiss him.

Because she sold pot, she was sometimes invited to parties. At one house party, she was sitting on a couch next to two boys from her school's swim team who began talking about a girl from a rival school with whom one of them had had sex. They talked about how her teeth had ruined a blowjob, how they'd tried anal sex in a movie-theater parking lot. As they described her, Mallory realized they were talking about one of Hannah's public-school friends, a girl she'd met before. She wondered whether there were other boys elsewhere who talked about Hannah this way; wondering this, Mallory felt far away from Hannah, as if Hannah was a character in a film and not her longtime friend. The boys talked so excitedly about sex with this girl that their voices grew loud and raucous. They looked over at Mallory, who smiled and nodded. One of the boys waved his hand in the air as if to say, *She's fine, she's nobody.* She herself had not yet had sex but thought that when she did, she would not want anyone to know about it.

Another night, she attended a cast party for people involved in her school's play. That semester, they had performed *The Laramie Project*, about a real boy from Wyoming, Matthew Shepard, who'd been beaten, tied to a fence, and left for dead. She'd been invited to the party by a boy who ran the lighting board, a frequent customer of hers, who had also invited her to watch the show from his booth earlier that evening. She couldn't imagine anyone wanting to party after working on such a depressing play; they all seemed to see the show as fiction.

At the party, she played Apples to Apples with her classmates, who had just smoked the pot they bought from her. They talked about, and scoffed at, a new rule at their school, put in place as a result of their performing *The Laramie Project*, that barred anyone from using the word "gay" in a derogatory way, as a synonym for "sissy" or "lame." While they spoke, a girl in the kitchen had started to dance without pants on, and everyone went to watch, including Mallory, who felt compelled to look away but feared doing so would be more conspicuous. The girl was wearing red-and-white-striped underwear dotted with cherries. Mallory felt her face get hot, and when the dance was done, she walked upstairs to use the bathroom. She avoided looking at herself in the mirror, imagining how awful it would feel to be beaten and left tied to a fence.

❦

Just after Hannah finished her senior year of high school, she threw a party at her house. Her parents were out of town. It was June, and two months later, Hannah would leave for Savannah College of Art and Design. Although as neighbors she and Mallory still saw each other, they had also grown apart.

Before the party, Mallory let Hannah dress her in a short plaid skirt and a black shirt buttoned just below her bra. Hannah did Mallory's makeup and straightened her hair, and as Hannah got dressed, Mallory looked at herself in front of a large mirror in Mrs. Allard's bedroom. She practiced pouting, the way Hannah had with torn-out magazine ads, but couldn't stop herself from looking cartoonishly sad. Still, she became aroused looking at herself, not because she thought she was all that pretty now but because she suspected someday that someone else would see this about her.

A boy Hannah was seeing at the time, Andrew, had a friend he was bringing to the party. Mallory was a junior in high school; by then, she had kissed a few friends of Hannah's boyfriends and had even come close to having sex with one. She couldn't get wet, but the boy had thought his dick was too big to fit inside her, and Mallory had allowed him to think this.

Andrew's friend was named Ian. His face had a benevolence to it, though it was pocked with acne. He wore a *Night of the Living Dead* T-shirt underneath an unbuttoned flannel. The shirt said, THEY'RE COMING TO GET YOU, BARBARA, but the overshirt hung in such a way that only EY'RE MIN GET BAR showed. Mallory thought it was more than a little unfair that she had to get dolled up to meet him.

For a while, she enjoyed Ian's company. They drank rum and Coke by the kitchen sink and talked about their favorite horror films. Periodically, Mallory watched Hannah, who was standing next to the girl whom Mallory had overheard the boys from her own school's swim team talk about. The girl was wearing a short skirt too, along with knee-high boots. She laughed a lot, and throughout her own conversation with Ian, Mallory found herself trying to laugh that way, too. Mallory thought the girl was pretty and pictured her doing the things the boys said she did. Then she tried to picture herself doing those things, but as she did this, she imagined the girl and Hannah laughing at her.

Another boy at the party approached Mallory to buy an eighth. After she sold it to him, Ian, who had watched the exchange, said, "So you, like, sell drugs?"

"It's only weed," Mallory said. "I do it mostly to buy books and rent movies."

"Why not get a job?"

"I have one of those, too." Mallory worked at the Hallmark Store in the mall, a few stores down from the clothing boutique where Hannah worked.

"Still," said Ian. "I mean, come on." Mallory imagined how she must have appeared in his head. She felt hideous and excused herself upstairs.

She went into Mrs. Allard's bedroom. She'd wandered in there on occasion when Hannah's parents weren't home. Mrs. Allard read a lot; she was the librarian at the same high school where Mallory's mother worked as a guidance counselor, though the two women had never been as close as their daughters once were. Mrs. Allard had plenty of bookshelves, but she left a lot of books scattered throughout the house. Sometimes, Mallory stole them, reading them herself before putting them back where they'd been.

On Mrs. Allard's armoire that night was Kazuo Ishiguro's *Never Let Me Go*. Mallory brought the book with her onto Mrs. Allard's bed, turned on the nearby pole lamp, and began reading.

Sometime later, the door, which she hadn't closed all the way, creaked open.

It was Wednesday. He jumped onto the bed with her. He was a big dog and looked both somber and regal standing beside her. Mallory gripped his paw, which felt fragile despite his imposing stature. As she began to pet him, he lay down next to her. She rested her head on him and heard the soft murmur of his heart. Mallory went back to the Ishiguro book and continued to smooth Wednesday's fur. After a while, he shut his eyes. Mallory's hand rose and fell with his breath. The sensation was comforting and made her sleepy. Soon, she shut her eyes, too.

She woke periodically over the next couple of hours, read, and went back to bed. At some point, she got up, shut the door, and locked it. When she finally woke for good, the house was quiet. She saw she had drooled on Mrs. Allard's pillow and so flipped it over. Wednesday was still next to her. Apologizing to him, she brushed the sleep from herself and went back downstairs. She had slept through the party; there was no one left.

It was just after one in the morning. Hannah was sitting

outside on her back deck. She was sketching the backyard, including the aboveground pool and the large tree that hung over it, in a notebook. Since it was early summer, the tree had bloomed with a lumbering fullness, and Mallory thought to herself how funny it was that in the warmer months the water was less exposed to the sun than it was during the winter, as if the pool itself preferred the coolness, and the tree, knowing this, protected it from the heat and the light. Hannah was still drunk, and her drawing was off. Mallory joined her, and together they drank from a big bottle of water. The night was warm and balmy, the thrumming of cicadas the only sound. Two lanterns affixed to the house's façade cast champagne-colored light over them. Hannah's upper lip was wet with whiskey and sweat.

"I honestly didn't know you were still here," said Hannah.

"I fell asleep upstairs. I tried."

Hannah laughed. "I know. I'm glad you're here." She stopped sketching and flipped to the next page in the notebook. She began drawing Mallory. "How was Ian?"

Mallory tried to sit up straight to look more ladylike. "Who?" Then she said, "Where's whatshisface?"

"We're not actually dating anymore. What's the point?"

"Because you're leaving?"

"I'm sort of seeing someone else." Hannah hesitated. "Don't tell anyone."

"Who would I tell?"

Hannah smiled. "True." She tipped her head to concede that point. She told Mallory that she was secretly seeing a chef from an Italian restaurant nearby. They'd met when she ate there with her parents. Her father had told the waiter to give his compliments to the chef, who came out and slipped his number to Hannah without her parents seeing. He was thirty-one.

"Do your parents know?" asked Mallory.

"God, no," said Hannah. "No one knows. That's the best thing about it." She threw her head back with a kind of ecstasy that reminded Mallory of the man masturbating in the pharmacy parking lot many years earlier. "When I'm with him, it's like no one else exists. I don't think about anything else. There's just him. And, you know, I never have to introduce him to anyone. It's great—what could someone say or do besides ruin it?"

Mallory felt jealous. She didn't know if it was the covetous kind of jealousy or if it was envy. She understood Hannah's wish to keep her relationship hidden; their own friendship had been so intensely private in the beginning that even being out in public together had felt, to Mallory, like a threat.

Later that night, Mallory got in Hannah's bed, even though Hannah had a guest room, and even though Mallory lived next door. The bed was a four-poster, with a mesh canopy that looked like a mosquito net. Since she'd already napped in Mrs. Allard's room, she wasn't at all tired. She wasn't even drunk.

As Hannah climbed in beside Mallory, she laughed, which made Mallory laugh, though she didn't know what they were laughing at. They turned to face each other. Hannah's eyes fluttered. Before she had gotten into bed, Hannah had forced herself to vomit; still tipsy and tired, she had just rinsed her mouth out with coconut rum, and now her breath came in waves of rotten tropical fruit. She said, "Sometimes I lie like this with him. He gets so focused on me, and I'm like, 'You could do this with any girl you wanted—any woman.'"

"But it's you."

"But it's me. You get it." Hannah licked her lips. "I love that I can tell you these things." She whispered this despite them being so close and alone. Her lips were chapped and sticky. She brought them to Mallory's, and as their lips met, Mallory's body stiffened. Then it slackened. She put her hand on Hannah's waist, but before long Hannah pulled away and fell asleep. The wantonness of the kiss made Mallory feel weightless, like she was floating, yet that night she lay awake staring at the mesh net that hung above them with the sense that she was caught up in it.

⤜

For days after the kiss, Mallory felt giddy and electric. On her days off from work, she sat and read on the patio under the sun and allowed herself to be enveloped by the tremendous verdancy of her backyard, the limb-spreading sycamores and flowering dogwoods, everything so green the world seemed to throb.

That summer she continued to work full time as a sales associate at the Hallmark Store. The job was easy and quiet and offered a discount on candles and cards. The store was especially slow in summer. Mallory read the "Sorry for Your Loss" cards as if they were little vignettes to which she could attach characters and scenes. During the ample downtime, she drew cartoons on the back of blank receipt paper.

Hannah still worked at the clothing store nearby, trying to earn as much money as she could before going off to college. On a day the two of them were both working, they took their lunch break together at the food court. Hannah ate half a salad. She said nothing of the kiss or the chef. In fact, Hannah hardly talked at all. They spoke briefly about customers that had annoyed them and then fell quiet. Hannah pushed the food around her plate with a dreamy expression on her face. She was, Mallory knew, thinking about the chef. The currents of their secretive relationship were so strong they pulled Hannah away from Mallory and the rest of the world. Mallory wanted to feel this way about someone someday, though she suspected she already knew what it was like.

Mallory was in the midst of ringing up a customer one afternoon when Andrew, the boy Hannah had broken up with earlier in the summer, walked in. He was with his mother. He sniffed some of the candles as his mother stood in front of the condolence cards. Mallory watched his face react to the different scents; he seemed to particularly dislike clean linen. After tiring of this, he went to find his mother but saw Mallory behind the counter.

"I didn't know you worked here," he said once he got to the register. "It's funny to see you."

"It's funny to see you, too," she said.

He pretended to browse the candy beneath the cash wrap. "How's Hannah?"

"She's fine. She's working a few stores down if you want to see her. Who died?"

He looked at her, taken back. "What?"

"Your mom is looking at condolence cards."

"Oh," he said. "An old coworker of hers."

"Sorry if that was intrusive."

"No, I don't care." He flicked his eyes in his mother's direction, then up at the camera behind Mallory. "Hey," he said, "are you holding?"

"Here? No way."

Andrew laughed. "I can't believe you do that."

"Rich kids," she said. "I also take their discarded textbooks from the hallways at school and resell them on Amazon."

"Hannah always said you were funny."

It depressed Mallory to hear someone talk about Hannah in the past tense. All summer she had felt Hannah fading from her life, as if each day a new part of Hannah peeled away and flew off to Georgia.

Andrew invited her to his pickup roller hockey game the next night. Mallory told him she would go. Most nights, Mallory had little to do but read at home. She liked doing this, loved it even, but also liked an excuse to do anything else. Whenever she was out, however, she wished she were back in bed by herself with a book.

❧

Mallory had never watched hockey before and found herself enraptured by its fluid grace: the skaters' constant movement back and forth, the orange puck skimming across the asphalt like a rock chucked sideways at a lake. The small crowd was gathered on steel bleachers and consisted of the players' parents, their siblings, their friends, some girls. Whenever either team scored, the boys gave each other high fives and hard, gruff hugs. To herself, Mallory laughed at how seriously everyone took the game. She wondered,

Do I care about anything that much? She loved art; yet there was nothing she delighted in that she could share the way Andrew and his friends shared the pleasure of sport.

In his car after the game, Andrew asked her if she had any weed.

She said, "Wasn't that why you wanted me to come?"

"You don't like hockey?"

"I don't know. I guess it was more fun than I expected. How much do you want?"

"Can I have a friend discount?"

"Are we friends?"

A look of thrift and want passed between them. "Do you want to hang out?"

In her car, she followed him back to his house. They went into his basement, where, for forty dollars, she sold him an eighth. He grabbed a bowl from a tackle box and took a hit before putting on his PlayStation. He handed her a controller, and they played a racing game. A woman with big breasts barely held in by a bikini began each race by waving a flag.

"Has Hannah said anything about me?" Andrew asked.

"Not really. I'm sorry. Is that better or worse?"

"I don't know."

"I don't think she wants to date anyone since she's leaving."

"We're all leaving."

"I'm not. Not yet at least."

After the third race, he began to kiss her, sliding his tongue into her mouth as she lay back against the sofa's armrest. As they continued to kiss, he pressed the full weight of his body into her. It was so unlike the kiss she shared with Hannah earlier that summer, the lightness of it replaced with a sudden and forceful hunger that felt as though it flattened her; she couldn't dwell on her own pleasure, or the lack of it, since his was so present.

After he finished, he said his mouth was dry. He got up to get a drink and came back with two pouches of Capri Sun. He stabbed the top of the juice with the straw's sharp end and sucked. He drank juice the way he smoked pot, puckering his lips. Mallory drank hers.

It had not been so bad. It hurt only a little; the lubrication from the condom he put on had helped. She was glad to have gotten it over with. And for a moment, she had been the pretty one.

Back at her house, Mallory stripped off her clothes and took a long shower. She turned the water hotter and hotter until it scalded her. She couldn't see anything else amidst the steam. The only good part of what had occurred, she thought, was that it didn't matter; she would probably never see him again, and no one would ever know. With nothing but this secret, she could have stayed in the fog until the end of time.

֍

At the end of August, Hannah left for college. From her mother's window, Mallory watched Hannah load her mother's Jeep before the two of them drove off, leaving Mallory to feel as though she was an ogling ghost, watching the world move forward without her.

Dejected and jilted, Mallory started watching pornography and having online sex. At first, the latter was meant to pass the time; in the evenings when she wasn't at work, time that felt almost interminable to her, she'd sit for hours in the basement in front of the family computer. She had never really masturbated before and didn't know how to do it, so she saw sitting in a dark room sending lewd messages to another person in a different dark room like a game, like *Minesweeper* or solitaire.

Her interest in porn began as an accident. She illegally downloaded numerous movies, but one of the files she found was the "adult" parody of the film she was really looking for. She watched it over and over. Mostly it was funny, the production values surprisingly high, but seeing such explicit sex in front of her made her feel so aroused that she sometimes put her tongue on the computer screen, leaving kaleidoscopic contrails of spit on the naked bodies. She downloaded more of the videos, which gave her something to say in her private chats, and changed all the file names. If they were somehow found by her parents, she could claim she was looking for the actual films.

Doing this was also a way to pass the time while Mallory, who didn't want to come across as needy, waited for Hannah to message her on AIM. But those messages never came. After seven years of close friendship, Hannah had forgotten about her. Throughout September and October, Mallory sulked around the house, sad to have truly lost what was once such a large part of her life.

It was hard to hide her feelings in the house, especially from her mother, who, now that she appeared to be healthy, seemed newly attuned to her daughter's sorrow.

One October night, a group of kids in hooded sweatshirts broke into Mrs. Allard's Jeep, which was parked outside in the driveway. The sound of the boys had woken up Mallory's mother at two thirty in the morning. Through her bedroom window—because Mallory's father snored, her parents often slept in separate rooms—Mallory's mother watched as the boys fiddled with the doors of the car, laughing and laughing with no hang-ups whatsoever over committing a crime. One of the boys even dribbled a basketball. They had not been trying to steal the car itself, just what was inside of it: the TomTom GPS that Mrs. Allard kept in its holder above the dashboard. When the doors didn't open on their own, the boys passed the basketball back and forth between themselves, even trying trick passes: behind the back, through the legs. They lobbed the ball over the Jeep, which sat helplessly. This went on for maybe ten minutes before one of the boys took two tiny objects out of his backpack. The first he laid down on the ground. The second, a small mallet, he used to smash the first thing, which shattered like ceramic. His friends watched him as he took the shard and threw it at the side window of the Jeep, like a dart. Almost without sound, the glass fractured. The boys whooped and hollered. Mallory's mother was astounded.

The morning after, a police officer told Mallory's mother that the object was a spark plug, and that cracked porcelain could create a fine, precise point sharp enough to pierce the tempered glass of a car window. Mallory's mother thought the boys were very inventive and maybe deserved whatever was in the car. She didn't tell the officer—or Mrs. Allard—that she had seen it all.

Instead, she recounted this to Mallory that next day, just after the police left. Despite having witnessed a crime the previous night, Mallory's mother had slept untroubled and had woken with a deep feeling of gratification. When Mallory asked why her mother wasn't bothered by what happened, her mother said, "Because I know Hannah hurt you."

Mallory swelled with affection for her mother. She felt protected. Also, she found surprising delight in the fact that a middle-aged woman could be as secretive and petty as a teenage girl.

⋎

Autumn fell. Mallory felt, at first, soothed by October's spookiness, as if the atmosphere was matching her mood, but as November hit, an impending sense of perpetual dusk dawned on her. Even at its brightest, the sun seemed weak, like it had been trying to carry a late-night conversation on the cusp of sleep.

One temperate day in November, Mallory came home from school and found her father sitting at the kitchen table, his face sagged with seriousness. Her mother, he said, was in the hospital.

For the past few weeks, unbeknownst to Mallory, her mother had felt as though she couldn't breathe, having also what she thought were heart palpitations. At first, she thought these were panic attacks; she was an anxious woman and had been made even more so by surviving two cancers, the most recent of which had been four years earlier. Remission, Mallory's mother had said, was like sitting in a rowboat while waiting for a tidal wave.

She'd recently had a blood test done. Her bone marrow was no longer producing mature blood cells. That was the word Mallory's father used: "mature." Instead, her mother's body could only make cells that were immature, which meant that they couldn't function as they were supposed to. This terminology seemed so silly to Mallory that she had difficulty seeing the illness as serious.

Later that evening, Mallory's father drove her to see her mother. The sun was setting but still, somehow, shone. Through the passenger-side window, a sliver of light fell on Mallory's leg like a bug. Squinting, Mallory peeked into the other cars on the highway and wondered where they were all going. It vexed her to watch the world go on. There was a forced solitude to her heartache that felt surprising and cruel.

When they got to the hospital, they took the elevator to the oncology ward. There was nowhere for Mallory to divert her eyes; everything she saw reminded her of where she was. The green-white gloss of the walls and linoleum floors was so bright she recoiled.

Outside her mother's room was a set of plastic drawers containing paper gowns, masks, and latex gloves. They came in packages, like Halloween costumes. Mallory and her father had to wear them, the latter said, because her mother's body wasn't producing enough white blood cells to fight off infection, which left her vulnerable to outside germs. Once the masks and gowns and gloves were on, they looked at each other. Mallory thought then that the consequence of living so much of life through books and movies was that actual dramatic things felt unreal.

Her mother lay with tubes protruding from her arm, connected to a bag filled with viscous yellow fluid—platelets, her father said. Mallory's mother turned away when she saw her daughter. For seven years she had suffered mostly in silence; anytime someone else witnessed this distress she became resentful toward them.

"Of all the gin joints," Mallory said. *Casablanca* was her mother's favorite film, and a quote from it was all Mallory thought she could offer. Her mother turned back toward her and let out a tearful laugh, which made Mallory think of her aunt, her mother's sister, who'd been "the funny one." *What did it matter*, Mallory wondered now, *whether a woman was pretty or funny? She was fucked either way.*

Her mother's wariness did soften for a moment, though, and she invited Mallory to cozy up beside her in the hospital bed. Mallory's hands looked shockingly large next to her mother's. "I'm fine," her mother said. She mussed the hair on Mallory's head. "I'm fine," she said again.

⚘

Her mother spent most of November in and out of the hospital, but because of school and work, Mallory didn't visit that often. When she did, she would become nauseated by the fetid breath of her mother's room. The nurses, orderlies, and doctors started to recognize her and her father, like restaurant regulars.

At home, her mother's presence was as unnervingly uncertain as a flickering light. One Saturday morning, Mallory woke to the sound of her mother howling in agony over a severe headache. Mallory stayed in her bedroom until the sounds of anguish subsided. Later, though, she made her mother a cup of chamomile tea, and as her mother sat with the hot mug pressed against her temple, Mallory went to put hot water and rubbing alcohol on a clean dishrag, which her mother had done whenever Mallory had a migraine. She came back into the bedroom and draped it over her mother's face. She stood and looked down at her mother, feeling proud that she had proved adept at this gesture of adulthood, yet upset that she could not dwell on how sorry she felt for herself.

The hot compress, however, didn't help. "It's not working," her mother said. "Nothing works." She balled up the rag and threw it on the ground.

Another day, her mother became so dizzy that she stumbled and fell into the kitchen table. She braced her fall with her elbow, driving it into the table's surface, and cried out in pain. The near fall left a bruise that lasted for days. "Why won't it go away?" her mother said. Mallory was shocked by the question's childlike cry.

Mallory started to crave quiet. Even though it was getting colder, she began taking longer to walk home from school. The world unfurled itself for her. Eager, stubborn sunlight winnowed through the trees dotting the road she took on her way home. The long, naked branches of the trees hung over the street as if they were reaching out to touch one another across the road's width.

❦

By December, her mother's illness seemed to subside, but because of her immune system's sensitivity, she had taken more leave from her job. Mallory often came home from school and found her mother sitting in the living room watching sitcom reruns, or reading the liner notes to her favorite records as if they were little novels.

Once, Mallory found her mother sitting at the spinet piano they kept in the basement. When Mallory saw her, she was playing along with Carole King's *Tapestry*, which blared from the stereo. It was her mother's favorite record; she'd started taking piano lessons in 1971 when the album came out. This had also been the year she met Mallory's father on a blind date.

She had been at the hospital a day earlier; she had to go there still as an outpatient to receive blood transfusions. Now, at home, she was wearing a surgical mask and latex gloves. Watching her mother play piano wearing these things was, for Mallory, like looking at a work of surrealist art. Their life was a dream in which everything seemed slightly off-key.

Her mother had her eyes closed but opened them as Mallory entered the room. Mallory saw the lines of a smile on her face even through the mask. Her mother told her to sit beside her on the piano bench. As she did, her mother said, "You're home."

Mallory said, "You are, too."

They sat wordless, listening to the music. Between songs, the sound of her mother's breath was amplified by the mask. "It's Too Late" came on, a song Mallory had grown to love since her mother had played it so often. She watched her mother's gloved hands play along, plunking the little fill in between lines, but the lyrics seemed too sad to sing out loud—*one of us is changing, or maybe we just stopped trying*—so neither of them did.

❖

For Christmas Eve, Mallory and her parents went out to eat. On the wall next to them in the restaurant was a large mural made up of naked, faceless bodies painted yellow. They were figures without form, like something from a book on how to draw. All throughout the meal, Mallory and her mother stared at the stationary dance of the yellow bodies, whose movements, to

Mallory, seemed sexual and lithe. She didn't know what her mother saw in them, though when they were finished eating, and while her father went to use the bathroom, her mother peeled her eyes from the wall and said, "It feels like I haven't seen you in forever. Have you gotten bigger?"

Mallory shrugged and rubbed her stomach. "Maybe I should have skipped dessert."

"Funny girl." Her mother started singing lines from Jefferson Airplane: "*One pill makes you larger and one pill makes you small. And the ones that Mother gives you don't do anything at all*—that's because moms don't want to see their daughters grow up, so if you could please stop, that'd be great."

☙

On a cold, rainy day in January, Mallory was walking home from school when a car pulled up beside her. She'd been listening to Philip Glass's soundtrack to the movie *Candyman* and was sure she had been caught playing the air in front of her like an invisible piano. The car startled her.

Through the veil of rainfall, Mallory, who'd forgotten her umbrella, saw Mrs. Allard's Jeep. The car crawled as Mrs. Allard rolled the window down and offered Mallory a ride.

"Are you sure?" asked Mallory. "I'm all wet."

Mrs. Allard said, "You're going to catch a cold."

Despite its heft, the Jeep bounced and sagged as Mallory got in. "Thanks," she said. "Sorry."

The car smelled musty, like a costume shop. Inconspicuously, Mallory tried to sniff herself to see if it was her that smelled.

"What were you doing walking in the rain?" Mrs. Allard asked.

"I don't know. I don't really live that far from school."

Mrs. Allard, who was Mallory's next-door neighbor, laughed. "I know."

In all the years they'd known each other, Mallory had not once been alone with Mrs. Allard. They'd existed on the periphery of one another's lives.

"It's nice to see you," said Mallory. "It's been so long."

"It has! How are you?"

Mallory gestured at her wet self. She felt this conveyed the general state of her life. Mrs. Allard smiled.

"How's Hannah?"

"She's good." Mrs. Allard's voice went high and craggy. She scrunched her eyes to see through the poor visibility of the windshield. "She doesn't call as often as I'd like, but she's good. Mr. Allard and I had to get one of those instant-messenger programs on the computer in order to talk to her. It's the only form of communication she seems to use."

Mallory gave Mrs. Allard a half smile, thinking of how many wasted minutes she'd spent waiting for Hannah to message her. "Right, yeah."

"Have you not heard from her?"

"I haven't, no."

"Oh," Mrs. Allard said. "That makes me sad."

"Me, too."

Just before their street, Mrs. Allard pulled the Jeep over onto the road's shoulder. "Really, I mean it. It does make me sad. I'm surprised she hasn't said anything to me."

Mallory didn't know what bothered Mrs. Allard more: that her daughter had cut ties with the girl who'd once been her best friend or that her daughter hadn't told her. Mallory knew that Hannah used to share a lot with her mother—her first kiss, the first time she had sex, how she felt when stoned. Mallory wondered whether Hannah had ever told her mother about their kiss.

"There's probably a lot Hannah hasn't told you," Mallory said. She gave Mrs. Allard a cartoonishly toothy grimace that she hoped said, *Oops.*

Mrs. Allard laughed, which sounded shockingly incandescent against the day's dank gray. "You're probably right." She swatted the air in front of her as if she was clearing smoke. "Enough about her. How are you, really? I was so sad to hear about your mom."

Mrs. Allard's voice was suddenly consolatory, so uncannily like Mallory's own mother. It was as if all mothers sounded this way, like that vocal register belonged only to them.

Another car drove past them, appearing as a mirage at first. Mallory worked over what to say and lost track of the rest of the world. She told Mrs. Allard everything she knew about her mother's illness, though this wasn't much. As she spoke, she worried she was betraying her mother in some way—her mother preferred to keep her misfortune cloaked—but Mrs. Allard's sympathy in that moment seemed more significant than anything else.

They drove the rest of the way home. Before Mallory got out of the car, Mrs. Allard invited her to stop by sometime. "It was nice catching up," she said. "And, as you know, I'm not that far away."

Loneliness caught in Mallory's throat like the onset of a cold. She said, "Okay."

⌄

By February, her mother's condition had worsened. After breakfast one morning, her father sat himself down with a kind of plodding clumsiness on the couch beside her. It was a Saturday, and she was mindlessly watching a cartoon. Her father picked up the remote, muted the show, and asked her if she knew what a bone marrow transplant was. She shook her head; how would she? Her parents had elected not to go through with a bone marrow transplant, which, her father said, would have been too painful and dangerous. Mallory felt agitated: by her mother for being sick, her father for calling attention to it, herself for being unable to help.

She said, "So, nothing's changing?"

He took a deep breath in and then let it out. His lips quivered. The breath that contained whatever else he wanted to say became smoke, which lingered for a moment before dissipating. Her father unmuted the cartoon and got up off the couch.

⌄

While her mother was away, back in the hospital, Mallory saw and heard the lack of her more than she felt it. She saw it in the money her father left for dinner in case he didn't come home. She heard it in the second-hand tick of the kitchen clock, which sounded unnaturally loud in the empty house.

Each year on Valentine's Day, her mother let her stay home from school. This was because in first grade, Mallory had been the only girl in the class not to receive candy or a card, and so every year after that, the two of them played hooky and went for a movie and a fancy lunch. "My date," her mother would tell the waiter.

This year, however, her mother wasn't home. Mallory took the day off anyway. She thought to watch porn, but without the cover of night this felt pathetic, so she spent the afternoon lying in bed, reading comics and watching the dismal films that aired during the day.

At around five thirty, she wandered into her mother's bedroom and sat by the window overlooking the Allards' driveway. Her mother's bed looked and felt dolefully untouched. Mallory saw that Mrs. Allard was home, and a few minutes later, she went down and knocked on the Allards' door.

When Mrs. Allard opened it, Mallory let out a laugh. She looked down at the ground. She hadn't thought of what to say once she got there; she had just wanted someone else to see her.

"No one's home," she told Mrs. Allard, who invited her in.

It felt like a long time since Mallory had last been inside the Allards' house. She looked around to see if anything had changed, and the fact that nothing had seemed even more strange.

Mrs. Allard said, "Would you like a glass of wine?"

"No, thanks."

"It's okay if you do."

"I actually don't like the taste of it."

"It's an acquired taste."

"I guess I'll have a little."

In the kitchen, Mrs. Allard pulled two glasses from a cabinet above the sink. To retrieve the wine, however, she had to go outside into the garage, where the Allards kept their alcohol. She held up the bottle when she came back in. "Zinfandel," she said. The name made Mallory think of a fantasy land populated by fairies and elves.

Down a step from the kitchen was a sunroom, which had a dining area where the Allards ate most of their meals. Mallory and Mrs. Allard sat there together. Mrs. Allard asked if she still read comic books, and Mallory felt that the word "still" sounded harsh.

As a librarian, Mrs. Allard explained, she had noticed an uptick in interest around comics—"graphic novels" she called them—and she asked Mallory what her favorites were. There was one, Mallory told her, in which the devil gets fed up with ruling over Hell, so he bequeaths it to someone else, knowing that the keys to the kingdom would be fought over once news of his abdication spread throughout the world. Mallory spoke in a rush, excited to be talking about her favorite thing with someone else, excited to be talking about anything with someone else.

With her eyes cast down into the wineglass, she told Mrs. Allard that whenever she visited her mother, she would bring a comic book because the pages were urgent and colorful and could easily distract her. She said this to elicit sympathy, though it was true, but the rickety smile Mrs. Allard returned made her regret it.

"You probably don't want to talk about comics," Mallory said.

"I actually used to read them when I was a girl," Mrs. Allard said. "I grew up with three older brothers, and I would steal the issues of Superman comics they bought from the drugstore or that they got from their friends. I hated the feeling of being left out. But then no other girl was reading them, so I had to choose which thing to be left out of."

"I know that feeling."

"I remember I used to annoy my brothers by telling them that all those men leading their double lives were dumb, that their problems would go away if they just told someone who they were."

"But then the villains would come after them."

"Well, I didn't really believe it. I just said it to get a rise out of them. Believe me, in a house full of boys, I understood the need to keep things from other people."

Mallory pinched the stem of her empty glass. Mrs. Allard asked if she'd like a refill. Mallory gave her a crooked smile and said, "Okay."

They looked at each other as they took a sip.

"It's funny," said Mallory. "I used to steal the books that you left lying around the house."

Mrs. Allard beamed. "I know!"

"You do?"

"Oh, totally. I'm a very careful reader." She held up her hands, wiggling her fingers. "The books would be much more worn after you read them, and sometimes you didn't put them back where I knew I'd left them. As a librarian, that's kind of my thing."

"You didn't say anything."

"Why would I? I didn't want to embarrass you. And honestly, I was worried you'd stop."

Mallory became newly aware that the two of them were alone. Mr. Allard was away, as he was for most of the week. He worked in Connecticut at a logistics company—Hannah herself hadn't really known what that meant or what her father even did—and kept an apartment there. Mallory looked at Mrs. Allard and thought she must be lonely, too.

"Thank you," Mallory said, gesturing to her wineglass. "I'm alone a lot, so this was really nice."

"You're always welcome here," said Mrs. Allard.

Walking home from the Allards' that night, Mallory imagined that the sky itself was watching over her. The stars appeared to her like eyes, as if she specifically was now worthy of the universe's attention and care.

⌦

If her parents weren't home and she didn't have work, Mallory went to see Mrs. Allard. It became something to look forward to; talking about books and playing Scrabble while drinking wine gave her days purpose and shape.

When she wasn't with Mrs. Allard, she imagined Mrs. Allard was thinking about her, watching her—at school, at work, even in the shower or in bed. Mallory lived her day-to-day life as if under Mrs. Allard's constant assessment. This made her want to be a better version of herself—or if not better, then at least someone worth watching from afar.

Mrs. Allard made large pots of chili on Sundays, which she would heat up throughout the week. She was happy, she said, to have another mouth to feed. She'd missed this about cooking since Hannah left, being able to do it for someone else. One evening, Mallory helped her make split pea soup, a dish Mrs. Allard had learned to make from her husband's mother, though she said Hannah and Mr. Allard hated when she made it, that it paled in comparison to his mother's version. Mallory thought it tasted good. She thought it tasted even better since she had helped make it and Hannah and her father hadn't liked it. She brought her face to the bowl, breathing in the steam, and she felt her whole body thaw.

Watching Mallory inhale the soup's vapor, Mrs. Allard asked if she still sold pot.

Mallory was startled. She said, "You know about that?"

"Hannah told me. She told me you had this whole plan to buy it cheaply from the boy down the street and sell it to your private-school classmates for twice as much. Is that true? I think that's genius."

"She didn't like that I did it. She used to call me 'Scarface.' You know, it was her idea to start smoking it in the first place."

"I'll bet. She used to be a little weirdo."

"I remember."

"When she was little, all she wanted to do was read and draw. For a woman like me, that was the dream. Your mom must feel that way about you."

"I don't know," Mallory said. "I hope so."

"Well, for me, raising a well-read child was a big win. Whenever I saw her reading books for fun, I felt like I had won the lottery. But then she got older and started to lose all that weight, and she seemed less interested in books. She still did her homework and got perfect grades, so who am I to complain? If she drank or smoked pot, so what? If she had boyfriends, okay, that's normal. Her falling out of love with books felt like a real loss, though. I would look at her and feel that I was falling out of love with my own child. That must sound so terrible."

Mallory didn't think that sounded like such a terrible thing to happen to Hannah, though she did worry her own mother would fall out of love with her one day soon. In fact, it terrified her that this was something that could happen. Each time she stepped into her mother's hospital room, Mallory felt they recognized one another less, and she dreaded being asked the question that felt more and more inevitable: *Who are you?*

❧

The next night she was free, Mallory brought over to Mrs. Allard a joint she'd rolled. They sat on lawn chairs in the garage with the door closed. Mrs. Allard placed the joint between her lips and sparked the lighter until it caught. Sucking in, she closed her eyes. The tip of the joint flared. She coughed as smoke billowed from her mouth. "It's been a while," she said.

"This is so funny," Mallory said. She laughed to show her commitment to making the scene a joke. She accepted the joint from Mrs. Allard, tasting Mrs. Allard's spit, which was briny like ocean water. As she smoked, she recalled drooling on Mrs. Allard's pillow and wondered whether Mrs. Allard ever noticed.

They passed the joint back and forth, each sucking on the wet end of it. It was as if they were just two friends hanging out. The joint shrank and shrank until it was almost gone. Mallory licked the tips of her fingers and pinched the lit end of the joint to snuff it out.

She offered Mrs. Allard the roach, but Mrs. Allard laughed

and declined. Mallory didn't know what to do with it so held it in her palm, the way she and Hannah used to trap lightning bugs.

In the quiet, Mrs. Allard looked serene. Her eyes fluttered, and a fine-spun, filmy smile settled on her lips. She looked the opposite of Mallory's own mother, whose every movement lately, no matter how slight, was long and drawn out.

Mrs. Allard gave Mallory a moony glance. "I know I said I fell out of love with my daughter, but I hope you know that isn't true. It's impossible, obviously. I really do miss her." She stretched her arms out wide in front of her. "Like, this much."

"I do, too," said Mallory. She had not been this high in years.

"I miss the sound of her hair dryer in the morning as she was getting ready for school. I miss the smell of her shampoo. I miss the sound of her scurrying up and down the stairs to make sure she hadn't forgotten anything."

A laugh rose up through Mallory, and she felt it leave her mouth. "She used to use the upstairs bathroom to put on her makeup because she thought she only looked good in that one. It was something about the lighting."

"That's so funny you say that. Or that she said that. I hate the way my teeth look in the downstairs mirror. They look so yellow."

Mallory ran her tongue over her own gums. She remembered why she hadn't smoked pot in so long; it stuffed her even further inside herself.

Using her hand as a shield, she glanced up at the light hanging above them. She said, "Speaking of lights, this one's so bright."

"I'm glad Hannah met you and that you two stayed friends

for so long," said Mrs. Allard. "I couldn't have dreamed up a better match."

Mallory became transfixed by the back of her hand, the part of herself she was supposed to know best. "She was the pretty one, and I was the funny one."

Mrs. Allard said, "You'll meet other pretty ones."

Mallory thought this was absurdly funny for a mother to say. Also, it was almost a compliment, though it wasn't as if Mrs. Allard was calling her pretty. "What does that even mean?"

"You're leaving for college soon. You'll meet other girls like you."

"Funny ones?"

Mrs. Allard laughed, but didn't say anything. The two of them sat there. A car drove past the house, and they heard its whoosh.

Being stoned in a suburban garage made Mallory think of the *Halloween* movies, and she had the sense of something sinister stalking her. When Mrs. Allard left her seat to let Wednesday out, Mallory waited only a minute before reentering the house, wanting another presence with her.

She wandered around the first floor from room to room before hearing something creak upstairs. She found Mrs. Allard in the second-floor bathroom, the door open, wiping off her makeup. Mallory stood in the doorway and watched Mrs. Allard do this. Still probably high, Mrs. Allard wiped her face, slow and indulgent. She said, "I don't know how truthful it is, but the lighting in here certainly seems more flattering."

Once she was done wiping off the makeup, she splashed water on her face. It was then she looked at Mallory, who was startled by Mrs. Allard's unvarnished prettiness. The cloth in Mrs. Allard's hand showed the smeared remnants of blush and eyeshadow, the detritus of everyday womanhood. It was a marvelous allowance, Mallory saw then, to be given a glimpse of what another woman kept hidden.

Mrs. Allard handed Mallory a towelette with makeup remover and made room for her in front of the mirror. When Mallory wiped away her own eyeliner, she stared at herself in the mirror. She looked at Mrs. Allard looking at her, and the two of them stood like this, bare before one another.

To the Mallory in the mirror, Mrs. Allard said, "You can tell me things."

"What things?"

"I don't know—how you are, really?" She brought her voice lower. "If you're interested in someone."

"There's no one in particular."

"But it's girls, right? You're, well, you know."

In a daze, Mallory considered the phrase "putting words in one's mouth" and almost wished Mrs. Allard would do just that. She said, "I don't know."

"It's okay," said Mrs. Allard. "You are who you are. I feel like I've always known and I feel like you've always known. I just want you to know now that you don't have to hide it from me."

"Okay," Mallory said, and she thought it could be. She luxuriated in Mrs. Allard's warmth, in this bathroom that was, she had to admit, wonderfully lit.

❧

Her mother needed brain surgery. They'd found a clot. Mallory thought of the joke—"It's not like it's brain surgery"—and actually laughed. Her life outside the Allards' house felt preposterous.

At the hospital, a nurse had shaved one side of her mother's head. Another nurse swabbed her mother's lips with glycerin when Mallory and her father came into the room. She was in a lot of pain just from this, so the nurse increased her morphine drip.

The nurse left the room with Mallory's father in tow. Mallory sat on a green couch next to the window. She looked out. It was, somehow, spring. The sun shone unusually for April; that it wasn't raining almost felt callous.

She'd brought a book with her—*Heart of Darkness*, which she was reading for school. She found it dull. Wishing instead that she had brought a comic, she looked down at the book so that she didn't have to watch her mother, whose mouth was moving though no words were coming out.

At home, alone, Mallory had developed a habit of reading aloud so that the house would not be so outlandishly soundless, and she found herself doing so now.

"Now when I was a little chap I had a passion for maps. I would look for hours at South America, or Africa, or Australia, and lose myself in all the glories of exploration. At that time there were many blank spaces on the earth, and when I saw one that looked particularly inviting on a map (but they all look that) I would put my finger on it and say, 'When I grow up I will go there . . . '"

Mallory wished Mrs. Allard would come pick her up in the Jeep. She wished Mrs. Allard would take her away toward the blank spaces on the earth.

Sometime later, Mallory's mother was prepped for surgery and rolled away. Mallory and her father sat in the waiting room outside where the operation was being performed. She picked up and flipped through various magazines but thought that none of the women in them could tell her what she wanted to know and so tossed them all back onto the table.

By then it was nearly midnight. On the television, CNN recapped the pope's recent visit to Ground Zero, where he lit a candle and said a prayer for the dead. Mallory looked over at her father, whose eyes were wide and glassy. He was glancing up at some spot on the ceiling, praying, maybe, or making calculations. His hair had grown long in the back; he hadn't had it cut in months.

"Hey, Dad," she said. When he turned toward her, she said, "Are you okay?"

"God, Mal," he said, "what are we going to do?"

Mallory was startled. It was as if she had been put in charge of a project she was incapable of completing. She turned back toward the television. The pope shook hands with the families of some of the people who perished in the attack. She said to her father, who was also half watching now, "I remember going to the pharmacy with Mom one time—this was like ten years ago—and there was that collection jar you could put your change into, you know, to support a children's cancer fund. Mom looked at the jar and said, 'The world makes it so hard to feel sorry for yourself.' I remember wanting to laugh, like she was saying, 'Forget those kids; what about me?'"

Her father cracked a smile. That was what it really did look like: a smirk fissuring his face. It was as if he hadn't smiled in so long that he had to retrain the muscles of his mouth to make that shape. He shifted in his seat, like he was gathering himself to tell her something interesting. He said, "Your grandmother said almost the same thing the last time she visited."

"What'd she say?"

"She tells anyone who'll listen how hard this all is for her. A doctor came in to check on your mom, and your grandmother asked him to check her own heart rate and blood pressure."

"I can totally see that happening."

"When an orderly came to bring your mom some food, your grandmother looked up at him and said, 'You know, I'm hungry. Can you bring me another one of those puddings?'"

Mallory winced. "I can see that, too."

Her father shook his head, as if he couldn't believe anything funny could be found here. "Today, another nurse saw me in the hallway and asked how my mother was doing."

"She thought Ruth was your mom?"

"She thought your mom was my mom."

"No," Mallory said.

"Yes," said her father.

Mallory's mother did look older; her once golden hair had become the color of coffee diluted by too much milk.

"That's awful," said Mallory. To her surprise, however, she still let out a laugh.

"I almost told your mom. Her being mistaken for a grandmother—especially given how her own mother is—might have shocked her right out of the bed."

They laughed again, and after their laughter died down, Mallory curled into a ball in her chair and fell asleep. She woke an hour later when the doctor who had performed the surgery came into the waiting room. He was young and strikingly handsome. Mallory had watched so many episodes of *ER* and *Grey's Anatomy* with her mother that she began to resent the doctor for having a dramatic and sexually robust life independent of saving her mother. The doctor said her mother was recovering. Mallory looked up, hopeful, but the doctor said, quickly, "From the surgery."

⌖

"It's been so nice spending time with you the last few weeks," Mrs. Allard said the next time they saw one another. "Sometimes it's felt like having Hannah back. Or at least, it's like having that time with Hannah back. But I've also just really loved talking with you."

They'd driven in the Jeep to a nearby park. The park was made up of wide, winding walkways and massive weeping willow trees.

"It has been nice," said Mallory. "Honestly, it's been the only good thing."

"I know. For me, too. Is everything okay?"

Mallory was looking out the window but got snagged by her own reflection. "I sort of hate this park. I mean, I've only been here once, when I was eleven, but it isn't a pleasant memory."

"A boy?"

"No, actually, a girl."

"At that age?"

"Oh, no," said Mallory, "it wasn't anything like that."

She told Mrs. Allard that she had come here for a class picnic in fifth grade. She'd been the only girl there without a bra. It was early June, and she wore a mesh T-shirt. Another girl in her class saw she had nothing on underneath and pulled Mallory aside to reprimand her, cupping her hands over her own breasts to make sure Mallory got the message. Mallory, hot with panic, spent the rest of the picnic with her arms wrapped around herself.

"I guess she was doing me a favor," said Mallory now. "I guess I needed to be dragged into womanhood. But I'd been sort of flat-chested, so it wasn't a pressing thing. I wore a bathing suit under my clothes until later that summer, when Hannah gave me one of her bras."

Mrs. Allard laughed once, a little absently, as if distracted. "She's coming back in a few weeks, for summer break. Obviously, that means we won't be seeing much of each other."

"Obviously," Mallory said, trying to hide how much this hurt her. While she had come to prize this private time with Mrs. Allard as something that was only theirs—only hers—she had also become, in this moment, weary over so much of her life becoming clouded by secrecy and loss.

The two of them sat in silence for a while. They looked outside the windshield, at a weeping willow whose branches, to Mallory, hung like a shy, uncertain girl's curtain of hair. Mallory pawed her own hair forward, hiding her right eye, wondering, *What's one more thing?*

"I'm sorry," said Mrs. Allard.

"It's okay," said Mallory. "I understand."

"I feel kind of bad, guilty even. No one should use another person to get over their own loneliness."

"Isn't that what we all do?"

Mrs. Allard was taken aback. "You're too young to think like that."

Mallory noticed now how the willow trees stood far apart from one another, as if they had self-consciously cordoned themselves off. She said, "I don't know what I am."

When she got home, Mallory smoked half a joint by herself on the back porch. It was cold, though the smoking numbed the chill in her bones. Soon, however, her heart began beating against her chest. She became dizzy. Whenever she closed her eyes, she felt as though she was on the verge of falling over. She lay down on the living room couch but could not avoid the world's swirl.

Still gripped with panic, she wobbled up the stairs and toward her mother's vacant room, toward the window that overlooked the Allards' driveway. There, by itself, sat the Jeep, which looked as though it had traveled so far even though it had hardly gone anywhere at all.

Storytime

After Mallory graduated from college, she moved to New York, where she worked three part-time jobs. She freelanced as a graphic designer, including being a "permalancer" for a small comic-book company; operated the chyron for a broadcast network's college-sports show; and reviewed children's books for a trade magazine. This last job she had gotten because of the woman, who'd sent the editor of the publication an email on Mallory's behalf.

Like many of her classmates, who'd been in college during the financial crash and graduated into its aftermath, Mallory scrounged just enough money to pay for food and rent. She lived in a two-bedroom railroad apartment with Joseph. To get to the kitchen, she had to walk through his bedroom; to get to the living room, he had to walk through hers. There were no locks on any of the doors, though Mallory didn't mind or care. He considered her sleeping with women sexy, and she allowed herself to be flattered by that.

Four years had passed since Mallory had last been with the woman, when they'd had their affair. Since then, Mallory had not seen much of her. They did exchange emails on occasion. The subject of these was usually "Checking In." The affair had ended with no drama or fanfare. At times, Mallory found this depressing, as if she'd been deprived of a proper dénouement, but it was hard to complain when the woman was a reference on her resumé.

Hardly a day or an hour passed when Mallory did not think of the woman. On walks around the reservoir in Central Park, she would listen to the same two podcast episodes on which the woman appeared, or to audio rips of her interviews on YouTube. While washing the dishes she learned rudimentary German. She read the woman's work over and over, a twenty-two-year-old flipping through picture books in the tiny bedroom she rented in Manhattan.

Just after their affair had ended, Mallory—who still, four years later, hadn't told anyone about it—fell into a thick funk. The world became as colorless for her as it had been during the time around her mother's death. During her junior year, she had gone to see a movie with some friends, a film everyone else loved except her. It was not that she found the film bad; she had no response to it at all. When she'd tried to recount her thoughts, it was as if memories of the movie she had just seen moments earlier had been surgically removed. She felt awful around other people; in a crowd, or even with just one other person, she would become convinced she was not capable of enjoying things to the same degree that everyone else seemed to enjoy them. It was as if she was constantly being told a funny joke and, while some part of her felt she should laugh, her body and mouth couldn't produce the laugh itself.

Sometimes she suspected she had given the best of herself to the woman, as if the fire of her life had burned most intensely when she was eighteen, and she no longer had enough energy to keep rekindling it. She had tried to date other people. In college, there was a girl on the rugby team, a hallmate of hers, and later there was a girl in the school's ROTC. In bed next to them, Mallory felt her body looked monstrously large.

Shortly after moving to New York, she started seeing a single mother she'd met online whose name was Emily. Mallory found out about Emily's daughter on their third date. She was speechless, but Emily said, "You don't have to say anything. You don't have to do anything. I'm not telling you this because I want or need your help."

Later that night, Emily told Mallory that her daughter had been the result of a teen pregnancy, an ordeal that had estranged her from the rest of her family.

They were at Mallory's apartment when Emily told her this. As Emily spoke, Mallory looked around her messy bedroom, the décor of which had come mostly from the college section of Target. Clothes were strewn on the ground. Garbage brimmed from a tiny can beside her desk. A poster of Wonder Woman she'd gotten at Comic Con adorned the wall. Mallory was frightened by the responsibility it would take to love someone with a child; she herself still felt like a child.

She tossed and turned that night, thinking of the woman from college, who had slept with a man in his forties when she herself was seventeen. The woman had mentioned this only once, almost offhandedly, as if it was a funny thing that had happened and she hardly thought of it at all. It occurred to Mallory now that what happened between that man and the woman might not have been good.

The morning after, Mallory walked Emily to the subway station and spent the rest of the day by herself. On the Upper East Side, the streets teemed with real lives. There were new parents pushing strollers, schoolchildren at play, grandmothers at rest. Dating women sometimes made Mallory feel lewd and fruitless. She imagined passersby asking, "And what do you add?"

Briefly, she considered what her life would be like parenting a child, or at least helping someone else raise one. With a pleasurable sense of vanity, she thought it might be nice to have a small version of herself. She would read *The Lord of the Rings* to the girl before bed as her own father had. She'd sing along with songs from the seventies as her mother did. But after a moment, these thoughts blew away like leaves in the wind. She would not want this girl growing up to be like her.

After things ended with Emily—"You're so young," Mallory was told—she had relationships with other women, whom she saw mostly in secret. It was difficult for her to date someone for more than a few months, and usually she would let whatever was there peter out. She was happiest on her own, when it was just her and the stories she told herself.

A few days a week, she brought her laptop and Wacom tablet to a café near her apartment. In addition to her freelance projects, she had started writing and illustrating a short graphic novel. The company she permalanced for published kids' comics, and she'd gotten the idea of making her own; the head of the company had said he would consider anything she wanted to show him. The story she had come up with, which she'd been working on since her sophomore year of college, was about a young girl who befriends a furry giant living in her backyard, the latter of whom gives the former a patch of its fur, which shields her from all harm as long as she doesn't take it off.

Rachel was a poet. She had an oval-shaped face and smooth, shoulder-length black hair. Her eyelashes were long; when she blinked, they created the impression that her eyes were dancing. When she smiled, which she did often, she kept her lips pressed together in a way that came across as playful and coy.

They were set up on a blind date by Joseph and his girlfriend, the latter of whom had modeled for a dating app's subway ad. They spent the first few minutes of their date laughing about this. In fact, on the train ride to the bar where she and Mallory met, Rachel had sat across from the image of Joseph's girlfriend, who sometimes got stopped on the street and asked out; Rachel wondered aloud how strange it must be to date someone who wasn't famous but could still be recognized while out and about. Mallory said she didn't know.

Rachel was from Texas and tried to hide her accent's twang, though it came out when she talked excitedly about certain things: her students, all of whom she seemed to love, and her childhood home, which sat alone on a dirt road, miles outside of town. With her phone, Rachel pulled up the address on Google

Maps and showed Mallory the view of it from the street. It was a one-story home—a "raised ranch," Rachel called it—with a lot of open land behind it. It was at once desolate and lovely. Mallory could imagine Rachel there. She could imagine herself there too, watching the sunset from the porch, and she felt comforted by this, as if it could happen tomorrow.

The longing with which Mallory looked at the photo must have been visible, because Rachel said, "It's nice, right?"

"It is," said Mallory. "It's kind of wonderful."

Rachel smiled, fluttering her eyes. Her lashes flicked skyward like a Rockette's high kick. Mallory thought a nice life, a good life, would consist of being the cause of that smile.

They talked for so long—about art and writing and trashy television—that they saw most of the tables around them change over. Mallory thought this meant the night was going well, yet at one point Rachel asked, because of Mallory's lack of eye contact, if she was being a bother. Mallory was taken aback, though she knew she stared off into space. This was not, she explained, because she was uninterested in what was being said but because of a childhood lazy eye; if she tried to look someone right in the eye while they were talking, she worried that her eye's drift was still discernible and she couldn't concentrate on the other person's words. She listened better, she said, if she was not looking at the person speaking.

She had never articulated this to someone else before and could not say, in that moment, why she had chosen Rachel to tell. She supposed it was because Rachel was the first to ask. Rachel offered a surprised smile, still tight-lipped but impish. She said it felt like the first true thing anyone had told her since she started dating in New York. This made Mallory feel warm and euphoric. She liked the version of herself that said true things.

⌄

Rachel taught undergrads as a way to finance her own graduate degree. Her writing and teaching schedule did not align all that well with Mallory's graveyard shift at the television studio, so they didn't see each other as often as normal couples seemed to. Rather than tarnishing their time together, these limited windows gave their relationship a specialness that both of them enjoyed. There was not enough time for troubles to arise.

Part of Rachel's own need for aloneness came, she eventually told Mallory, from a terrible relationship she'd had with a high school boyfriend. He'd taken her for long drives in his car and threatened to run them off the road if she didn't devote herself to him. He did this so frequently that she moved to New York primarily so she would never have to be in a car, even years after they'd broken up. She preferred to walk everywhere, and with her, Mallory experienced the city differently. With Rachel, places felt less like destinations than a map's blank spaces.

One night, Rachel took her to a bar in the East Village at which patrons weren't allowed to talk. The interior of the pub resembled a monastery. The walls were done up with absurdist, medievalesque murals, and Gregorian chant streamed softly from the speakers. The servers wore monk's robes.

The two of them drank Belgian beer, smiling at one another. At first, Mallory thought it was all a little ridiculous. She looked at Rachel, who wore large glasses yet peered overtop of them in a way that made her seem, despite the softness of her features, sardonic and judgmental. It made Mallory feel like she was being pranked.

Soon, however, the initial silliness of their surroundings started to dissipate. The bar's hushed warmth wrapped itself around Mallory. She took a sip of her drink and tasted every drop of it as it slid down her throat. She looked at the lips of Rachel's heart-shaped mouth, pressed together in a pout. Mallory felt very present. It was as though time had slowed, or stopped, and Mallory thought then of what the woman from college had once said about misery: that it was pleasing in its ability to make things stand still, which was why miserable people often did things that extended their misery. But, in that moment, Mallory wasn't miserable.

It was three months into her relationship with Rachel, after more than a year of living in the city, that Mallory saw the woman in person. Mallory had set up Google alerts with the woman's name, though it was, she had immediately learned, a common name. Coming across a reference to a woman who was not *the* woman jarred her. This was especially true since the woman's name was the password to Mallory's computer.

The woman had a reading scheduled at the Barnes and Noble near Mallory's apartment. It was for the bookstore's Storytime, which they held most Saturday mornings. Mallory thought it might please the woman to see she was living well in Yorkville, the place the woman herself had grown up in after immigrating to America. She thought it might make the woman proud. Also, she thought a plausibly accidental encounter would offer her—Mallory—some comfort, as if the only way to ensure the woman considered her at all was to be physically seen by her. Mallory was forever worried the woman would forget her.

Mallory was going to surprise the woman by just showing up

but then thought better of that; because of the nature of their past relationship, the shock of seeing Mallory might lead the woman to think she was being stalked. She sent the woman an email instead, saying she had seen her name on the store's event calendar. They arranged to meet for coffee at noon, after Storytime.

The morning of the woman's appearance, Mallory showered and put on makeup. She did this while watching a video of Joy, her college roommate, who was paying her way through law school by filming beauty tutorials for YouTube.

At a little after eleven, Mallory walked the six blocks to the bookstore. She browsed for a book to sit with that would impress the woman should the woman catch her with it. She eventually chose a Dostoevsky collection that contained both *The Double* and *The Gambler*, novellas she had seen on the woman's shelf.

She skipped the introduction to the book and went right to reading but was soon distracted by Tumblr and some magazine articles she had saved on her phone—this despite the Starbucks seating area being located next to the store's magazine rack. She didn't know how much time had passed this way until she saw the woman waiting at the coffee counter. Storytime had ended.

Mallory saw the back of the woman's head before anything else. It reminded her of the same view from the treadmill at the college gym where they had first seen one another. She became almost immediately and painfully nostalgic for the feeling of aloofness the affair had afforded her.

Leaving the Dostoevsky book at the table to save it, Mallory made her way to where the woman was standing. She tapped the woman on the shoulder, which made her feel pleasantly childlike. When the woman turned, however, she gave Mallory a look stuck more toward distress than delight.

"Mallory?" the woman said. Her eyes widened. "I'm sorry, I forgot we were supposed to meet today."

"Oh," said Mallory. Her body seemed heavier to her suddenly; she could feel how much of an imposition she had become. That her outsized anxiety over being forgotten was justified both vindicated and disquieted her. "That's okay, we can see each other some other time."

"No, no. I have some time now. Let me buy you a coffee."

The woman had ordered something called a "red eye." When Mallory asked what that was, the woman explained that it was a coffee with an extra shot of espresso. She asked Mallory what she wanted, but Mallory told her she'd already ordered.

"I have a seat," Mallory said, "if you'd like to sit." Before they went over to Mallory's spot, the woman poured milk into her coffee cup. Mallory, who had learned back in college that the woman typically drank her coffee black, asked her about it.

The woman stirred in the milk. "Black coffee yellows the teeth," she said. "I went out with a man a few weeks ago who kept looking at my mouth and running his tongue over his own gums. He told me that my teeth had a tint. Can you believe that?"

"What a jerk," said Mallory, who desperately wanted to ask about what sounded like a date. But she didn't. She wondered whether this meant the woman was single or if she had just cavalierly admitted to another affair.

They took a seat at the table where Mallory had just been reading. The Dostoevsky book slumped open like a banana peel.

The woman picked it up and saw what page Mallory was on. "You haven't gotten very far," she said.

"I just started a few minutes ago." Mallory was nervous in a way she hadn't been in a long time, in a way that only the woman could make her. She was nervous in a way she had missed.

"You know," said the woman, "Dostoevsky gambled away his wedding ring." She looked down at her own ringless finger. The skin, Mallory noticed, was lighter where the band had been. "I am very sorry I forgot about our meeting. My life feels far away from me at the moment." She held her hand out across the table and regarded it as if it were a foreign object. "My husband and I are getting divorced."

"I'm sorry," said Mallory. She was more surprised by this than she thought she'd be. The woman's divorce made Mallory feel that the world followed a logical, comprehensible order, yet despite this, Mallory's heart sank. She wanted the woman to be happy; her hopes for her own happiness seemed inextricably linked to the woman's.

Mallory reached her hand across the table and held the woman's as an act of consolation; she could offer that now. The woman tensed but allowed Mallory to touch her. This lasted only for a moment.

"What happened?" Mallory asked. "Do you want to talk about it?"

"No," said the woman. "And don't get married. The tax benefits aren't worth it."

"I'm not. I mean, I won't."

The woman's face softened. "How are you?"

"Fine," Mallory said, "but no one ever means that, right?"

She thought to tell the woman about Rachel, but revealing her own contentment seemed impolite, so she told the woman that she was working three part-time jobs. The woman perked up when Mallory mentioned being a chyron operator; she'd never heard of such work.

Mallory explained that she was responsible for putting the graphics on the screen during football and basketball games. She'd had to get training and certification for this, though all she really had to do was press a couple buttons at the right time. When Mallory revealed how much she made doing this, the woman laughed. It was absurd, said the woman, to be paid sixty dollars an hour to press a button. She said, "I feel like you have found a respectable method for stealing money."

"It's not as fun or easy as it seems," said Mallory. She told the woman that the show she worked on produced video segments and highlights for the live games' halftime shows and for the channel's morning shows, which meant she often had to stay at the studio until three or four in the morning, waiting for games to end on the West Coast. The stakes were high, since what they did was for live television, and many nights she and her coworkers took small doses of Adderall to stay focused and awake. When she got home, she would be too keyed up to sleep. "Honestly," she said, "I've been thinking about quitting. But seeing your reaction, that you find it fascinating, kind of makes me want to stay."

She looked at the woman then, and the woman smiled. Mallory still found the woman striking half a decade later. Her blond hair, parts of which had lightened to almost white, and the pronounced pouches under her eyes made her appear marvelously accomplished and wise. Mallory shifted in her seat, aroused by the muscle memory of having been in the woman's bed, a time when she felt best about herself—beautiful enough to ruin someone's life.

"It really is lovely to see you," the woman said. "I am glad you're doing well."

Mallory smiled with one half of her mouth, an upturned frown. "I know this might sound silly," she said, "but it hurts to know you're hurting."

"That's very kind of you to say. I often wonder how you think of me. Sometimes I worry you might not like me very much."

"How can you say that?" Mallory asked, genuinely aghast. "You changed my life."

Over the past few years, she had seen the woman's mark on almost everything she did or said, everything she drew or wrote or read, every encounter she had with another woman. Every movement she made still felt as though it was being performed for the woman's approval. She thought this had given her life a wonderful sense of direction.

"I supervised a student thesis last semester," the woman said now. "She reminded me so much of you. She was very funny. Looking at her, I thought, 'I want you to do well in life.'"

"That's nice," Mallory said. It was difficult to dull the jealous edge in her voice. The woman had said the same thing to her but had never allowed Mallory to be her student. "What was her thesis about?"

"It's not important," the woman said. There was a long pause. "I suppose I should tell you: I've accepted a job at another college. It's in Florida, in the sun. I'm leaving in a few months."

A lump arrived in Mallory's throat. She swallowed as if she might choke. It was not as if they saw each other often, or at all, yet the woman's leaving to teach somewhere else was a shock. That the woman would no longer be living in New York meant the thrilling possibility of seeing and being seen by her would be gone.

After a period of silence, the woman checked her cell phone and announced she had to leave the bookstore to run errands. She said, "I think I might see a movie." The woman liked to go to the movies alone, which Mallory had admired, but now she found herself upset by this. Mallory would have liked to see a movie with her. She would have liked to sit with the woman a little longer.

✧

Hours after she saw the woman at the bookstore, Mallory took the train to Brooklyn to see Rachel. When she arrived, they went into the bedroom—Rachel shared a one-bed apartment with another poet in her program, rotating who got to use the bed every couple of weeks—and closed the door. They sat on the bed. A table fan was trained on them, and Mallory let the cool air blow over her.

"I'm so happy you're here," Rachel said. She smiled with the apples of her cheeks. They made out hungrily; their relationship was still new enough that they felt deprived when they weren't together. Rachel's mouth tasted of cigarettes, a habit she had picked up from her mother, who had, she said, picked it up from her own mother. "I wrote a lot today, and after I finished, I felt this weird loneliness and started talking to myself. It's so jarring to get out of that space."

Mallory said, "My day has been jarring too. I had coffee with someone I knew in college, a professor actually. She was sort of like a mentor to me. I found out today that she's leaving to teach in Florida. I couldn't believe that she could just get up and go. I don't even think she was going to tell me."

"I'm sorry. Were you close?"

"That makes it sound as if a relative of mine died." Mallory remembered what it was like to tell Rachel about her mother, how easy it had been, how Rachel's eyes had looked so willingly open, as if her whole being was shifting to allow in Mallory's grief. "But I do feel weird about it. It sort of feels like this hole that I didn't know was there has widened even more."

"But you'll still keep in touch with her, right? If you're not her student anymore, what does it matter that she's leaving New York?"

Mallory thought about this. It was, she supposed, a good question. "The only times we really spoke were when we saw each other in person. I just feel like I haven't learned everything from her that I could."

Rachel, who was a professor herself, understood this. "What did she teach?"

"Children's literature. She's from Germany, and other students called her Eva Braun. They didn't think she was very nice."

"I've had many female teachers like that. They had reputations for being mean, but I think that's mostly sexism."

"I can see how she'd be perceived that way, but I just didn't see it."

"Oh," Rachel said, poking Mallory's belly, "you had a thing for her."

"I don't know," said Mallory. She imagined how light she might feel if someone else knew.

"I had a crush on my geology professor. He was pretty young and tried really hard to relate to us. It was a planetary geology course, and he'd show us these old sci-fi movies from the fifties that didn't have anything to do with what we were learning. It was kind of cute."

"Cute," Mallory echoed. She felt then that Rachel wouldn't understand. Many students had innocent crushes on professors, but Mallory felt what she had done was dramatic and deviant. Before, this thought would have given Mallory a sense of superiority. Now, she felt like a loser. Yet she didn't know exactly what she had lost.

Later, they watched a movie in bed together. Mallory was distracted for almost the entire runtime. She imagined herself instead beside the woman in a cool, darkened theater, an electric tension between them. This turned her on, and she began to kiss Rachel, who was shirtless and in only underwear since the small apartment was so hot. They took turns going down on each other, and afterwards, slick with spit and sweat, took a cold shower together, playfully jostling for the water's relief but shrieking like girls at its chill.

While Mallory lay naked reading part of a comic book on her phone, Rachel finished getting ready for bed. Despite being a smoker, she had a forty-five-minute skincare routine. Soon, she rejoined Mallory, opening her Moleskine notebook to read back over what she had written earlier that day. She'd told Mallory once that she loved to read her work while other people were in the room; if she could imagine them stealing a peek at what she wrote and she wasn't embarrassed then she knew she had written something good.

As Rachel read, Mallory checked her email. There was one from the woman.

> It was lovely seeing you today. I'm sorry again that I forgot. In a few weeks, I will be house-sitting for some friends of mine in Salem, Massachusetts, while they're on vacation. You can come visit one weekend, if you'd like. Take a break from pressing your button.

Mallory stared so long at the message that Rachel asked what was wrong. Without thinking, Mallory showed her the phone. She said, "It's that professor I told you about."

"That's so weird," said Rachel. "What does she mean that she 'forgot'?"

"It was kind of embarrassing. We agreed to meet at the bookstore and, when I showed up, she didn't remember we were supposed to meet. She was there anyway, for a reading."

"My niece calls it 'Old-timer's.' I love that."

"She's not that old."

"Are you going to go? Massachusetts is kind of far."

"I don't know," Mallory said, though she already knew she was.

Despite Mallory having manufactured their meeting that morning, their reentering each other's lives at this time felt like fate. That the woman had forgotten about the meeting and still appeared made this, for Mallory, even more true. Mallory had once thought her life could be clearly split between before and after the affair with the woman, but she began to think that there was no before or after; the arc of their lives had forever bent toward each other, the way trees on opposite sides of the road touched and entangled their leaves.

Things between her and the woman had ended with a bizarre abruptness at the bookstore, and Mallory couldn't bear that their encounter—their relationship—could wind up that way. She couldn't bear that their story could end.

Mallory took an Amtrak train to Boston and then a regional train to Salem. She caught a cab that brought her to the house where the woman was staying, a five-minute drive from downtown. The day was hot and bright. The easygoing sun gave Salem a surreal feel; she felt as though she was at the start of a horror film.

In an email, the woman had instructed her to use the back door. Mallory walked past the driveway, which lay on the right side of the house, and came to a gate. Beyond the gate lay a small yard with a concrete patio and a wrought-iron picnic table. The gate's lock was unlatched, but she had difficulty pulling it from its hinge.

It was then the woman came out of the house. She was carrying a glass of lemonade. Sunlight glinted off the cubes of ice. The woman wore large sunglasses in which Mallory saw herself unable to open the gate. The woman said, "The owners put a charm on the house to ward off troublemakers."

Tired from the long journey, Mallory could not readily

produce a retort. She said, "It's so strange to see Salem in the sun. It feels like it should be permanently overcast."

"Like seeing Pripyat on a cloudless day," the woman said. "Like spending Halloween in Tahiti."

As the woman pulled open the gate, Mallory caught a whiff of the lemonade. It smelled of alcohol. They gave each other a hug, and the woman kissed her on the cheek. The parameters of this weekend stay baffled Mallory. The woman was sort of an ex-lover, sort of a former teacher, sort of a friend—yet not really any of those things. Not being able to define what they were to each other had satisfied Mallory once, but now she felt as though she had been given a wrapped gift whose contents remained mysterious even after shaking the box. She wasn't even sure she wanted what was inside.

The house they were staying in was two stories tall and more vertical than wide. This meant the hallways and stairwell were narrow. On the first floor was an eat-in kitchen and a living-room area with a nonfunctional fireplace made of exposed brick. The two bedrooms were on the second floor, which was decorated in a nautical theme, the walls soft blue and off-white. A painting of a docked ship hung in the hallway.

"Is Salem some sort of beach town?" Mallory asked the woman. "I feel like I'm in *Jaws*."

"I find it charming. I've been able to get a lot of work done here."

"Are you under its spell?"

"Cute," said the woman.

She showed Mallory to the bedroom where the latter would be staying. Inside, there was a window that overlooked only the house next door. Through it, Mallory could see a turned-on television but not the person watching it. The screen showed a prescription-drug commercial in which a contented woman went about her daily tasks even as the cloud of some indeterminate illness loomed over her. Mallory left her bag in the room and followed the woman back downstairs.

They sat at the table in the backyard. The woman fixed Mallory a spiked lemonade without asking her if she wanted alcohol. It was strong. "I'm glad you're here," said the woman. "I'm glad I could do this for you. How many jobs do you have again?"

"Three."

"Three," the woman repeated. "And you must be working on a book of some sort."

"How did you know?"

"What is it about?"

"Isn't that a bit like asking a woman her age?"

"Would you like me to read it?"

"Actually, I brought the first draft of it with me, if you'd like to look at it." She felt then that, despite the woman having asked, she was bullying the woman into flipping through it. "Not now, I mean. Whenever."

"I would love to," said the woman. "But yes, not right now."

Mallory was glad the woman hadn't wanted to look at her work now. The woman was too truthful, her opinion meant so much, and Mallory didn't think she could bear an entire weekend if the woman didn't love it.

The woman asked how Mallory had passed the time on the train. Mallory told her that she'd read *The Double*, though she didn't tell the woman that she had fallen asleep after thirty pages and, upon waking, did not return to the book. Instead, she read four volumes of a fantasy comic about famous fairy-tale characters living secretly in modern-day Manhattan.

Mallory said, "I've never been to New England before."

She'd found that revealing her greenness to women often endeared her to them. Sometimes, while having a drink with someone, or even in bed, she would lie and say she hadn't done or seen something when she had. Once, she'd gone out on a date with a barista who had just gotten back from London, a city Mallory had visited with her parents when she was young; the barista was so excited about her trip that Mallory sensed she should pretend not to know anything about it.

In this case, however, it was true that Mallory had never before been north of New York.

"I love it here," said the woman. "To me, this is America." The woman relaxed back in her chair and sipped her lemonade. She did not look like someone in the midst of a divorce. It made Mallory happy that, in the face of all the terrible things the woman's life had contained, the woman could still find awe.

"Everything I know about this place comes from books," said Mallory. "I just recently reread *The Scarlet Letter*. It's so good. I don't think I appreciated it in high school."

"I can't imagine why you would like it," said the woman. Without seeing the woman's eyes, her tone was hard to make out. Mallory did like the book much more since she herself had had an affair with someone who was married. "You should read *The House of the Seven Gables*. The actual house is here, you know."

Mallory took out her phone and typed the title into a note. The woman asked what she was doing.

"I write down everything you tell me to read," Mallory said. "In college, I used to go back to my dorm and write down the things you said to me—about books, and writing, and marriage, and adulthood."

At first the woman did not appear surprised by this. She looked off into the distance, though there really was no distance, just another identical-looking house with a small patio similar to the one on which they sat. When she glanced back at Mallory, she said, "That's not the comfort you think it is."

Mallory felt skinned. "I meant it as a compliment."

"I know you did."

Mallory tried to brighten her voice in a way that belied the sense of dread that had crept in. "You say such funny things."

⌇

For dinner that night, she and the woman went for pizza. It felt nice to stroll alongside the woman in public, as if they were friends, perhaps equals. But then Mallory wondered whether their being equals would make her less interesting to the woman. The woman already had a lot of friends.

On the way to the restaurant, they passed a school. There was a sign in front of the main building that read STILL MAKING HISTORY. Earlier that day, in the taxi, she had passed a cop car with an image of a witch on the driver-side door. This struck Mallory as profoundly strange; Salem's past made for an eerie point of pride. She wanted to call the woman's attention to the sign. She wanted to say, *It's like what you once said about Germany, that in order to go about their lives people had to forget what happened.* But she was worried now that her memory of this detail would make things between them uncomfortable.

They soon arrived at a main street intersection. The twilit evening was warm. People spilled in and out of cafés and shops. It looked like any main street in America. *How far away*, Mallory found herself wondering, *were the women hanged, the man crushed by stone?* They crossed the street and walked another two blocks to the pizza place, which sat next to a witchcraft-themed tour company promising family-friendly fun.

In the restaurant, they sat at a booth along the back wall. Despite it being summer, the warmth of the wood-fired stove was soothing. The two of them ordered beer, and when the glasses came, they clinked them together. Sharing a beer with the woman made Mallory feel cozy and blissful.

"Thank you for having me here," Mallory said. She tried to say this quietly enough that the other patrons wouldn't hear the raw gratitude in her voice.

"I know how hard it is to get away," the woman said.

"I was supposed to work tonight and tomorrow. It feels nice not to have to go in. These are the first vacation days I've taken."

"It's hourly pay, though, isn't it? Aren't you losing money?"

"It's okay. The button will be there when I get back."

The woman laughed. "Dinner is on me then."

In the opposite corner of the room, by a large window, sat two girls about Mallory's age. They were whispering and leaned forward to hear one another. One of them, the one facing Mallory, wore a black shirt that read SALEM, ESTABLISHED 1626 and had the same image of the witch and the broomstick seen on the town's police cars.

Mallory turned her attention to the menu, carefully studying it, trying to choose something that would both fill her and not cost the woman too much money. Yet when the waiter came to take their order, the woman asked for a salad and a soppressata pizza to split. When he left, the woman said, "Is that okay? It's the best thing here."

Mallory said it was fine. She was glad she didn't have to make a choice. She continued to stare at the two girls. The girl with the Salem shirt had her arm on the table, reaching across it as if in invitation to be touched by the other girl. Mallory looked so long at them that the woman turned to see what she was staring at. Feeling avaricious, she turned her attention back to the woman.

"I don't know why I find it so funny," Mallory said, "that this town is obsessed with its own history. It's just not a great history."

"They make so much money from it," the woman said, "so why not be gleeful?"

"Gleeful," Mallory repeated. "It's kind of shameful, isn't it?"

The woman thought for a moment. She looked back at the girls Mallory had been staring at, then said, "The couple whose house we are staying in—they're two men. One of them has a tattoo of a pink triangle on his leg. He's proud of it. He wears shorts whenever he can, just to show it off."

"A pink triangle? Like, the Holocaust thing?"

"Yes. And this is a man who lost a lot of loved ones."

Mallory lowered her voice. "Because of AIDS?"

The woman said, "He has been with his partner for a long time, and they don't plan on getting married even now that it's legal. They're onto something."

"Why wouldn't they?"

"When you are constantly told you're different, sometimes all you want to do is go off and be different. Marriage is boring. He jokes now about how much he misses being oppressed, how thrilling it felt when a relationship with another man was taboo. He says this so often that I don't actually think he is joking."

"Honestly," Mallory said, "I sort of understand what he means. Don't you?"

"Of course. There is no better sex than the kind no one knows you're having."

Mallory felt her face flush. When the waiter arrived with the food, Mallory avoided his eyes. The girls in the corner had finished their meal and were holding hands, waiting for the check. Mallory rubbernecked at their naked affection like it was a car wreck.

She glanced back at the pizza placed before her. She was hungry, but she waited for the woman to take a portion first. The woman put a slice on her plate and cut it into two slivers. After doing so, she sighed, as if this had been a great exertion on her part. Mallory took a slice and cut it in half just as the woman did. She hadn't ever cut a slice of pizza before but, suddenly, putting the whole slice in her mouth seemed barbaric.

On dates, Mallory would usually ask whatever woman she was with lots of questions so there would not be a dip in energy or interest. She wanted to do this now, even though this wasn't a date, but all she could think of were people like her dying in the streets and being blamed for their own deaths. Having been born at the end of the eighties, this kind of hysteria was almost hard for her to fathom, though she could recall being scared as a kid over the possibility that she could catch and spread the disease. Until now, she hadn't thought of how that possibility still haunted her.

After dinner, when they went back to the place where they were staying, passing the school that was "still making history," Mallory felt the entirety of the house, already strange to her, had shifted in some imperceptible way. She kept thinking how two men lived here together, slept here together, and that they invited others into that home.

Waking the next morning, Mallory walked downstairs into the kitchen and found a note next to a half-full French press. The note said: *Coffee here. Yogurt in the fridge. Working all day. See you later.*

Mallory could see, through a screen door, the woman sitting outside. She wondered when later was. The woman had set up the patio table to be a makeshift workspace, and it was clear she did not want to be disturbed.

Befuddled by the woman's remoteness, Mallory poured some of the coffee into a skull-shaped mug, heated it up in the microwave, and plucked a peach yogurt from the fridge. She sat alone at the kitchen table, watching the woman work outside, shoveling small dollops of the yogurt into her mouth. Indulgently, she licked the spoon clean, testing to see if she could catch the woman's attention, as if the only thing that could rouse the woman was the performance of a lewd act. But Mallory realized she did not want to get the woman's attention this way, so she stopped.

On the table was a picture book called *Duck, Death, and the Tulip.* It must have been something the woman was reading for inspiration or curiosity; despite the woman's profession, it made Mallory feel funny to see such a book in a house without kids.

She flipped through it. The pages were large. The drawings were delightful in a dainty way. Death stood before Duck wearing what looked like a caftan, a blackened flower held in his hand. "I've been close all your life," Death told Duck. They struck up a nice friendship, but in the end, Duck died. "That's life," Death said.

Done with breakfast, Mallory, who'd been unprepared for the picture book's depressing wallop, stood before the sink and washed her mug. Instead of washing the spoon, she let it fall from her grasp. It clanged against the steel basin. She turned to look at the woman, who was now looking back at her. The woman smiled, waved, but did not get up from her seat outside. She was wearing a brace on her wrist designed, Mallory knew, to alleviate the symptoms of arthritis or carpal tunnel. They shared the habit of cracking their knuckles, which Mallory also shared with her father, who often wore the same brace around the house. Mallory washed the spoon and went back into her bedroom.

Was this, Mallory wondered, what the woman had planned when she invited her here? Mallory had hoped the woman would show her around town. She hoped to see how the woman lived free from the burden of her marriage and whether Mallory, now that she was older, could fit into that life. She had hoped the two of them could be something like friends.

For a moment, Mallory mulled over getting back in bed. She unbuttoned her pants to take them off, not wanting the outside germs of her jeans to contaminate the sheets. But then, glancing out the window, she remembered she was in Salem, a town that was almost mythical in her mind. Sitting on the floor, she opened her computer and looked at a map of the downtown. She packed her sketchbook in her bag and set out to see the sights.

To exit the house, however, Mallory had to walk by where the woman was sitting on the patio. The woman looked up at her, quickly shutting the notebook in which she was sketching.

"I think I'm going to walk around," said Mallory, hoping the woman would put away her work and join her.

"You should," said the woman. "Maybe you will see some ghosts."

"Do you want to come? I don't really know where I'm going."

"The ghosts only show when you're alone."

❧

By herself, she followed signs to the House of the Seven Gables, which seemed as good a place to start as any, though it took her longer than expected to get there, about a half hour's walk from where she and the woman were staying. The house itself was painted an ominous black, which made it look frightening and alien, yet a part of Mallory also found its abnormality agreeable against the rest of the town's bucolic normalcy. Wishing she had at least read the summary of *The House of the Seven Gables* on Wikipedia first, she felt sucked into paying for a self-guided tour. The house, she learned, had been built in 1668 by a wealthy merchant named John Turner, but the first room she encountered upon entering was a reproduction of one of the first rooms described in Hawthorne's novel, published in the 1850s; the property, Mallory soon gathered, was actually two disparate things rolled into one: the residence of actual, historical families and a re-creation of the setting from the fiction book. The grandson of the wealthy merchant had squandered the family fortune and had to sell the house to someone else, a man named Ingersoll, who ultimately died—along with his son, his heir—of yellow fever, leaving the house to his daughter, Susanna, a cousin of Nathaniel Hawthorne with whom the author would later visit in order to learn about the history of the house, which he then used as the basis for the book. After the novel's publication, the house became more famous for having been written about than having been lived in. Mallory's mind spun trying to straighten out how the house she was now walking through was based on the book that was based on the house. She tried to untangle this as she entered a large, formal dining room, stopping in front of a portrait of a plain-looking girl. Despite the bags under her eyes, she looked young; Mallory couldn't quite place her age. The portrait before her was of Susanna Ingersoll, the daughter who'd inherited the house after her father and brother died. She was born in the house and died in it unmarried; she had referred to the property as her own private prison, a fact that saddened Mallory and made her think of the woman, who'd spent so much of her childhood feeling confined in a small living space with a sick loved one, her sister, and had developed a deep need to flee, something the two of them—Mallory and the woman—had in common. This was why it felt so comforting to be in the woman's presence, like being the only two people at a party who don't know anyone else there, and why she felt so bereft when the woman announced she was headed to Florida. She had wanted to reach out to the woman and beg her not to go, feeling as she had when she could no longer see Mrs. Allard and what she felt at her mother's funeral, a dejected and resentful sense of being left wanting, a need to know how they could leave when she still felt so incomplete. Recently, though, there were times when she wondered what her life would be like without the possibility of the woman in it, times when she wished the woman's voice in her ear would quiet, when she wished she could look at herself without trying to see through the woman's eyes, could take a step without wondering what the woman would do and how she would do it. She had once gotten so much pleasure thinking of herself as a character in the woman's life, as if she weren't really a person at all but words on a page awaiting further instructions, yet in the years since their affair she just felt blank. Looking around at the house she was in now, stuck somewhere between real and imaginary, Mallory started to feel like she was in a dream, her head heavy with the soggy logic of fiction and history and swimming with ghosts, so she left the house and walked through the property's gardens, which were peaceful and lovely and offered her an almost immediate relief. Contrasted with the dark color of the house, beautiful flowers bloomed as if in spite. Strolling behind the house to the edge of the property, she came across a large lawn being set up for what looked like a wedding ceremony, the backdrop of which was Salem Harbor. She leaned against a railing that overlooked the harbor, watching the ebb and flow of the water, the boats floating close to one another, and she thought of the saying "like ships passing in the night." In the noontime sun, she wondered why this phrase didn't also apply to ships during the day; weren't ships just as lonesome in the light? Mallory was starting to sweat, since even standing near the water it was hot, and so she went to a café two blocks away to buy an iced coffee. While she was waiting in line, she checked her phone, surprised that the woman hadn't texted or emailed her, and surprised, too, at her surprise over this. A part of her swelled with gratitude for the woman, who'd allowed Mallory to visit her here while also allowing Mallory to see the place for herself, untroubled with someone else's experience of it. That was Mallory's whole life—a private viewing of the world, like visiting a museum after hours—and what the woman had given her, both this weekend and when they had conducted their affair more than five years earlier, was an exhilarating sense of exemption. But there was another part of her that was very tired of all this privacy, this being alone. Something caged inside her had cried out to the woman, to Hannah and Mrs. Allard, *I will keep your secrets*, but the secrets she carried felt heavier and heavier every day, and she wasn't sure she could handle any more weight. Drinking her iced coffee, she walked west from where she was and came upon the Witch Trials Memorial, a somber area despite the shining sun, abutted as it was by an old burial ground. The memorial consisted of granite benches inscribed with names Mallory hadn't thought of as belonging to real people; to her they were characters in *The Crucible*. Mallory was watching a child place a small flower next to one of the names when a shriek of "Oh my god" cut through the park's quiet. Mallory looked up and saw the two girls from the pizza place the night before. At first, she thought she imagined them; she had thought about them last night while lying in bed and was shocked to see them during the day. One of them held a large camera with a zoom lens, and they were both peering into the camera's display screen. The one not holding the camera glanced up from it and apologized to the other people in the park. The camera, Mallory heard one of the girls say, had activated its facial-recognition mode while capturing one of the headstones, as if they'd caught a ghost. Mallory thought this was funny, a story worth repeating, one she wished she could share. She was, however, also annoyed at the way the girls called attention to themselves; so much of her experience with desire had been to hide it. Yet once the girls had moved on to another part of the cemetery, their merriment subsiding, Mallory felt compelled to follow them, curious what they were going to do next, trailing behind them as they walked until they came to what looked like a church, the sign above which said SALEM WITCH MUSEUM in unsettling yellow letters. Mallory followed them into the museum, which, she learned, housed an animatronic stage show telling the story of the trials. The girls bought two tickets, and Mallory bought one for herself. The show occurred every half hour, so they had to wait a few minutes, and while they waited, one of the girls looked up and caught Mallory's gaze, flashing Mallory a smile, which Mallory attempted to return without revealing how nervous she felt over possibly being recognized as one of them. She remembered the affection they had shown one another in the restaurant the night before, and it felt now as if they were extending that affection to her, and yet, to Mallory, their togetherness stood in stark contrast to her solitude, and the longer she was exposed to them, the more uneasy she became, as if feeling a throat tickle that could burst into a cough. The theater opened, and they went in. The space in which the show was staged was dark and dank, with chairs and benches in the middle encircled by raised platforms, which, once the light dimmed and the show began, depicted different scenes from the trials. The girls had been younger in real life than they were in *The Crucible*, and Mallory wondered why, for the play, Arthur Miller had made one of the girls, Abigail Williams, the main character's mistress, but Mallory supposed the leap from bookish child to concubine did not seem far somehow. They were impressionable young girls who took a story too far. As the audience watched, one of the girls whom Mallory had followed rested her head on the other's shoulder. They held each other in a way that made Mallory desperately miss Rachel and made her think about the time she had taken an early-morning taxi all the way from Rachel's apartment in Brooklyn back to her own place in upper Manhattan, a ride that took her alongside the FDR Drive by the East River, which had looked breathtaking as the day was breaking, a view that suggested freedom, despite Mallory's hands worrying the seatbelt strap that held her in place, and when she closed her eyes, Mallory had imagined she wasn't by herself but cozying up to Rachel in the taxi's backseat, the two of them looking out at the morning together.

Now, in the darkened theater of the Witch Museum, she felt homesick and alone.

When Mallory returned to the house, she found the woman sitting in the kitchen. Despite her homesickness, it was a relief to see the woman after a day of being on her own. With the woman, she still had the sense of safely contracting. Her thoughts and desires dwindled to a more manageable size.

"It's nice to have someone here with me who can entertain herself," the woman said. She was reading an issue of the trade magazine for which Mallory wrote reviews of children's books—the job the woman had helped Mallory get.

"As an only child," Mallory said, "I'm used to it. I didn't really have a lot of friends growing up, either."

"I didn't start making friends until adulthood. It's the only good time to have them. Everyone has lives of their own, so you can have a friend for every occasion. There's the couple friend, the single friend, the tennis friend, the work friend, the city friend, the country friend."

Mallory said, "Are we friends?"

The woman said, "I'd like to think so."

Mallory smiled. She wondered what category of friend she'd fall under. The young friend, maybe.

On the kitchen counter were canvas grocery bags filled with fresh vegetables. Mallory asked if she could help make dinner, but the woman waved her off. "You're my guest," the woman said. "Besides, I don't mind cooking for someone else, but I would much prefer not to cook *with* someone else."

"I know what you mean," Mallory said. "I've gotten used to cooking for myself in my little kitchen, and if I ever invite a date over to cook for them, it's like I only want to see them once the food is served."

The woman glanced at her, giving her an inquisitive grin. Mallory had the impression the woman was just now imagining her cooking in some small Manhattan kitchen, making a meal for another girl, frying an egg on a slanted stove. It was dizzying, Mallory felt, that performing an act of adulthood could still make her appear as a child in the woman's eyes.

Mallory went upstairs to the bedroom in which she was staying. She stripped down to her underwear, thinking she would take a shower, but got caught up texting Rachel about her day. She told Rachel about the House of the Seven Gables and about the two girls whose camera captured a ghost. Her thumbs tapped against the phone screen in a way that eventually began to irritate her the more she did it; she wanted Rachel here with her. She fantasized about returning with Rachel one day soon and regretted that she had experienced Salem first with someone else— which, really, had been no one else.

She put her clothes on and walked back downstairs and into

the kitchen. Music came from the woman's laptop, which sat on the kitchen table. It was tuned to a Pandora radio station playing doo-wop hits. The woman's hips swayed with the music as she cooked. Mallory had never seen this side of the woman before—had never heard the woman listen to music before—and wondered if they really were becoming friends.

With the vegetables she had bought from the store, the woman was making a tofu stir-fry. Mallory laughed. This had been the first and only meal the woman had ever made for her, nearly five years ago, on the night of their first kiss.

"Is this the only dish you know how to make?" Mallory said.

The woman was using a silicone spatula to push around the ingredients in the pan. She placed the spatula down on a folded paper towel beside the stove. "I've made this for you before?"

Mallory listened to the sauce's fizzle. She watched the peppers wilt in the heat. "You made it the first time I went to your house."

The woman said, "You're making me feel demented." She laughed, and so did Mallory, but Mallory felt as though she had been singing along with the radio and had the music abruptly shut off midsong.

They ate dinner outside on the patio. They drank a bottle of wine Mallory had brought—a Gewürztraminer, an inside joke the woman had also forgotten—and when that was done, the woman opened another one. Mallory hadn't wanted any more to drink but thought it would be rude to refuse.

The woman asked her what she saw on her walk. Mallory began telling her about the House of the Seven Gables, but it became clear that the woman knew all about it, so Mallory stopped. Instead, she told her about the girls in the graveyard and what they captured on their camera, though she did not tell the woman who the girls were or that she'd followed them across town.

"Maybe you were right," said Mallory. "The ghosts do come out when you're alone."

"Loneliness always seems so luxurious," the woman slurred. "All the time I want to be by myself but then when I am, I desperately want someone else around."

"That was my whole childhood. Does that feeling ever go away?"

"Does it ever go away?" the woman repeated. It was as if she was asking herself the question. "You know when you are sitting by yourself on the train and someone walks by, and even though there aren't many seats free, the person doesn't sit with you? You are relieved that you have the space to yourself, but also, you think, 'Why didn't this person want to sit with me?' I don't think that ever goes away."

Mallory felt a familiar clutch in her chest. It was the ache she'd experienced whenever the woman articulated something about Mallory's life for which Mallory herself hadn't known the right words. Her face shriveled into a wince.

"What?" asked the woman.

"You say these things about your life, and it's like you're talking about me. It's like you're reaching inside me and plucking out a thought or a feeling I didn't even know I had. I know that probably sounds weird, but that's why I used to write down everything you said. You made my life make sense."

The woman said, "I am glad you can look back and remember the good things about our time together."

Mallory was taken aback. "I don't remember any of it being bad."

"I was married. And you were so much younger than me. Running around like that was awful."

"I'm sorry," said Mallory, though she felt discounted. Many nights she had been kept awake by the thought that their relationship meant something different or held less weight for the woman than it did for her. This was almost certainly true, Mallory knew, yet it still stung.

The woman sighed. "You don't have to apologize. Sometimes you meet the wrong person at the right time, or the right person at the wrong time."

Mallory hoped she was the latter, though she understood that there was not, and never had been, a right time for the two of them. But she did not want to think of herself as a "wrong" person.

"You look offended," the woman said.

"I'm not," Mallory said. She shook her head to erase whatever daft expression was on her face.

She thought the woman might say something nice that would reaffirm Mallory's specialness. Instead, the woman said, "I'm afraid of being alone and afraid that is the only way I know how to be."

☙

After dinner, Mallory finally went to take a shower. In the bathroom, she tried to slide the bolt of the door's lock through its rusted slot, but it got caught. Each try to lock the door produced a loud clanking sound, which she was sure could be heard outside the bathroom and throughout the house. She thought the clang might appear annoyingly aggressive to the woman, so she left the door unlocked.

She turned on the shower, and while the water warmed, she took off her clothes. She folded them on the toilet seat, nice and neat. She got in the shower. The water pressure was strong. It was unlike the pressure in her own apartment in New York, a downpour to a drip. Despite its strength, she flipped a notch on the showerhead; that it even had options made the experience feel opulent.

In the midst of shampooing her hair, she heard a knock on the door. The woman's voice called, "Can I come in?"

Mallory peeled back the curtain. Before she answered, the door opened, and the woman stood before her. The woman wore a towel, the twisted knot of which rested just above her breast. Instinctively, Mallory yanked the curtain closed. This then made her feel embarrassed; the woman had seen her naked many times, and Mallory now worried her awkwardness, along with her thunderous inability to lock the door, came off as dismissal.

"Is everything okay?" Mallory asked. "Am I taking too long?"

"You just got in, didn't you? Can I join you?"

"Oh," said Mallory. "Okay."

The woman shrugged off her towel and stepped into the shower. They had never seen one another without makeup. Mallory assumed she looked awful and felt, at first, the anxiety of being seen as ugly by someone she had spent so much time trying to impress. But then the unexpected dread of actually being desired now descended on her.

The woman peeled a tuft of hair from Mallory's forehead. "Can I have some water?"

Mallory stepped aside. Water cascaded onto the woman and then on down the drain. Mallory watched; it was as hypnotic as watching rain slide down a windowpane. She did not feel like an active participant in what was happening.

"You're staring," said the woman.

"Sorry," said Mallory. But the woman was smiling. She wanted to be watched. This was what Mallory offered; if nothing else, the woman would find flattery in Mallory's eyes.

The woman was still beautiful and fit. As a reflex, Mallory wrapped one arm around her own less taut waist and the other across her chest. She said, "How do you still look like that?"

"It's hard out there," said the woman. "Men my age want girls like you."

The woman reached out and touched Mallory's breast, running a thumb across Mallory's nipple, which became erect. Standing naked before the woman after a long time apart and being touched in this impassive way struck her dumb. She suddenly saw herself as an impressionable young girl who had taken a story too far.

As Mallory stood dazed, trapped in the narrow shower, the woman leaned forward and kissed her. Mallory returned the kiss; no part of her was able to resist it. The falling water felt like it was no longer washing anything away. It enveloped the two of them like heavy rain. This might have made Mallory swoon five years earlier, but in that half decade their lives had changed. It was Mallory now who had something to lose. Thinking of Rachel, she became queasy.

"I'm sorry," she said to the woman, pushing herself away. "I can't."

She tried to get out of the shower without causing too much of a scene, but she'd had a lot of wine at dinner and slipped stepping out of the tub. She nearly fell to the floor. She couldn't recall a time when she was more embarrassed. All her ridiculous desires had led to such a careless life and messy results. She took a towel from the rack and put it on.

She was about to leave the bathroom when the woman shut off the shower. "Mallory," she said, "what's going on?" She grabbed her own towel from the rack and fastened it around herself. As she sat down on the lip of the tub, which Mallory had just tripped over, the towel almost came undone. The woman clutched at the cloth with desperation, holding it firmly in place, as if being exposed or vulnerable in this moment would have been the most awful thing.

Sitting herself on the closed toilet seat, Mallory said, "I'm seeing someone."

"What do you mean," the woman asked, "like a therapist?"

"No."

"Oh, you mean you're dating someone. Why didn't you tell me?"

"I don't know. It didn't come up."

"Mallory," the woman said. Out of the woman's mouth now, her name contained none of the sweetness it once had.

Mallory hung her head. She wished it would roll right off. It felt heavy as she lifted it. "We hadn't seen each other for such a long time. Our writing to each other was less frequent. And you literally forgot we were even supposed to meet at the bookstore. When you told me you were moving, I thought, 'This is it.' I wanted to see you before you left. It felt like the last time, and I was worried you wouldn't want me to come if you knew I was with someone."

"Given our history," said the woman, "you must have expected something to happen here."

"I don't know. I wasn't sure you still felt that way about me. I thought we were friends."

"We aren't friends."

Mallory shivered at the woman's unhesitant chilliness. "I have no idea what we are. I have no idea what I even mean to you, if anything." Her voice cracked, which made her realize it had been raised. "You must know how I feel about you."

"You make it sound as though I do not care about you at all. And clearly, I do not know how you feel about me."

"If someone were to ask me about the time I was happiest, I would tell them it was with you, though I still haven't told anyone. We met at the end of what was the worst year of my life. I never thought I'd meet someone who felt the same way about me as I did about them, especially not a woman like you. But at dinner, you said you were miserable then, and now I think I was totally wrong about that time, that how I remember it is not at all how it was, that I was just this stupid girl and you were just this miserable woman who wanted company." Mallory felt like a boulder rolling down an endless hill.

The woman gazed at her gravely. "I'm sorry you feel that way."

"Is that not how it was?"

"Well," said the woman, "of course I wanted company. But I wanted *your* company. And I could sense how much you wanted mine. I might not remember what I made for dinner one night, but I do remember being followed into the restroom. I remember someone coming to visit me in my office. I remember this same someone coming to my office even after we decided to stop seeing one another."

Mallory stared at her bare feet, which looked ridiculous now against the tiled floor of the bathroom. They looked like they weren't even hers. "You don't have to talk about me in the third person," she said. "I know I did those things. I know I'm guilty, too."

"No one needs to be guilty."

"You once said to me that we would have to live with what we did. Or don't you remember saying that, either?"

"Now you're simply being cruel."

This shocked Mallory. She did not want to be thought of as someone who could hurt someone else. She disliked confrontation; even now she was shaking.

The woman stood up and rubbed her backside. Sitting on the lip of the tub must have been uncomfortable, and Mallory felt sorry for the whole situation. But as the woman left the bathroom— "Get some rest," she told Mallory on the way out—Mallory began to think that if she had become a cruel person, it was the woman who had made her that way.

Mallory went into the guest bedroom. Still wrapped in her towel, Mallory lay curled in a ball on top of the covers. She was cold. There were messages from Rachel on her phone, but she didn't have the heart to read them. *I'm afraid of being alone and afraid that's the only way I know how to be.*

⌄

The next morning, the woman made breakfast for the two of them. "I feel bad about last night," she told Mallory. "I don't want you to be upset with me."

Breakfast was a soft-boiled egg, served in a shot glass, and buttered toast, which the woman had cut into strips. The woman offered milk for Mallory's coffee, but Mallory told her she still drank it black.

They ate on the patio. It was another sunny day in Salem. They were quiet. Mallory didn't know how to eat a soft-boiled egg. She didn't know what she was doing there or why she had come. She didn't know anything. She watched the woman crack the egg with a spoon and begin peeling away the shell. Inside, the yoke was runny. This seemed to please the woman, who took a piece of toast and dipped it in the egg. She waited for Mallory to do the same, but Mallory said she wasn't hungry.

"You should eat," the woman said. "It's a long trip back."

Mallory took a piece of plain toast and put a little bit of it into her mouth. When she was done chewing, she said, "I should have told you I was seeing someone."

"You should have, yes. I would not have rescinded the invitation. You were, and still are, an important part of my life. I always look forward to seeing you, to hearing your laugh. I am sorry if I haven't expressed my admiration for you."

"I know how hard it is to say things out loud."

"I do feel as though I have always been forthcoming with you. I told you about my sister. I told you about the man I slept with when I was young. Not even my husband knows about him."

"He doesn't?"

"I never wanted anyone else's thoughts about it. I was worried he would think I was fucked up."

It was startling, for Mallory, to hear the woman phrase it that way. It was even more startling to hear that the woman's teenage affair with an older man still affected her decades later. She'd told Mallory about it in such a nonchalant way, but clearly it still haunted her. Mallory thought she should feel proud that the woman had told only her about it but instead she felt unsettled.

In the period of silence that followed, the two of them watched as a brown-and-white rabbit hopped through the small yard before stopping in front of the chain-link fence. It was like something out of a storybook. The rabbit slid its head through one of the holes in the fence. Mallory felt heartbroken over how pathetic it looked with its head stuck. But somehow the rabbit shimmied its whole body—fatter than the fence's narrow opening—through the hole and popped out the other side. Mallory looked at the woman, who also sat astonished at the rabbit. It seemed like one of those things in nature that happened all the time but was hardly ever seen. Looking back at the space where the rabbit had just been, Mallory felt glad that the animal had prevailed, upset that it had tricked her into thinking it was trapped, and, finally, sad that it was no longer there.

Epilogue

FIVE YEARS LATER

The tiny house sat by itself toward the back of a four-acre farm. It was made mostly of glass and red wood. Grass grew around its black wheels. To Mallory, the house looked more like an unhitched train car than a living space. But through a large window she could see a café table with two chairs and an entire kitchenette: a stainless-steel dishwasher and microwave, a sink, a one-burner hotplate, an electric kettle, and a shelf lined with wineglasses and champagne flutes.

Mallory saw all this clearly even from the car pulling up to it. She got out and helped Caroline, the girl she was with—though they were both twenty-eight, so really, they were women—with her bag.

The weekend had been Mallory's idea. It was their first get-away as a couple. They'd met in January and had been seeing each other for almost six months. Through the winter they had cozied together in Caroline's bed and watched people play piano covers of pop songs on YouTube, and when the weather warmed, they avoided the city's heat by watching reviews of movies they felt guilty for never seeing. They were both homebodies who were more comfortable with physical intimacy than chitchat, sex a preferable form of expression, so they did not mind spending all their time in bed together. But Caroline lived in a basement apartment in Koreatown, and Mallory thought booking a tiny house in the Hudson Valley would allow them to do what they felt most comfortable doing while also letting themselves be enveloped by a vast and airy landscape.

They were tired from the two-hour drive. They toured the tiny house, Caroline taking pictures for Instagram, and collapsed onto the bed to take a nap. When they woke, Mallory made tofu stir-fry, which they ate at a picnic table outside the house. Caroline continued to take pictures on her phone, of what was around them but also of Mallory, who'd never really had her picture taken by someone she was dating. It was embarrassing and flattering all at once.

The descending sun tempered the day's heat into a sultry flush. Periodically, the two of them seemed to vanish into the immense and beautiful solitude of the open land. Love, thought Mallory, was a lot like getting lost alongside someone else.

Caroline looked very happy, and Mallory became pleased with herself for being the cause of it. She wanted never to be the reason that happiness evaporated.

"I've never been away with someone before," Caroline said. "With another girl, I mean. It's nice."

"It is," said Mallory. "I'm glad we're doing this."

"There are so many firsts in my life that I wish I had done with someone else. This is not one of those times, but do you know what I mean?"

"God, yes."

"The first vacation I ever took with someone I was dating—it was with a guy. I knew by then that I was gay, but I went with him anyway, to this oceanside villa in Montauk to watch the whales. He was really rich. It was just so easy to be sucked in."

Caroline had met this man, she explained, after she'd returned to America from Japan, where she'd taught English after college. As a hobby, she translated manga and anime online. She was what was called a "fansubber," which meant that she sometimes helped bring pirated versions of Japanese cartoons to an American audience by producing translated subtitles. She had become well-known in some online forums, where she spoke to other translators and fans. The man she dated was the latter. They had started talking online and, when they learned they were both living in New York, began to see one another in person.

"He was my first everything," Caroline said. "He was the first person I went on vacation with who wasn't family. He was the first person who I saw many of my now-favorite movies with. I had my first and only Michelin-starred meal with him, my first orgasm. At the time, I was happy to do all this with someone who seemed important—more important than I was, anyway."

Mallory was aware of how much Caroline was sharing, more than she had before, and though she herself wanted desperately to confess her relationship with the woman, which she still hadn't told anyone about, she sensed Caroline's need to lighten a burden from her own life.

"What made you think he was so important?" Mallory asked.

"He just had a lot of money. He had some high-powered finance job. He lived in a two-bedroom apartment by himself on

Central Park West. Like, he owned the apartment outright. When I was there, I felt like I was on a television set. I had a pretty low opinion of myself then, and being with him made me feel like somebody. But it was such a sham. I didn't even tell anyone about him because I knew it wasn't real." Caroline stopped. "Is it okay if I tell you all this?"

"I love that you're telling me all this. Why wouldn't it be?"

"It's just that I haven't said this out loud to anyone before. No one knows, so it feels funny."

"I can keep a secret."

"I don't want it to be a secret. And I'm actually a little tired of keeping it."

The sun had nearly set by then. The vibrant green of the trees had become almost blue. Soon the two of them would get a fire going, which would be nice, and Mallory now found herself gazing into the unlit fire pit, as if her intense wishing to set it ablaze would make it so.

"You know," Caroline said, "there's this word in Japanese, *boketto*, which is when you stare off into the distance in such a way that you lose track of yourself. Sometimes I think we do that when we become too aware of ourselves, and it's our brain's way of saying, 'Let me be, let me rest!'"

Mallory turned to look back at Caroline. She smiled and said, "We should start a fire."

"Okay," said Caroline.

The owner of the house kept a stack of wood specifically for use with the fire pit. Mallory lifted the pit's mesh lid and placed a couple logs onto the grill. Caroline went inside to get sweaters for the two of them. She brought out a book of matches, struck one, and held it to the wood. Before long, a fire roared to life. They sat beside one another on Adirondack chairs and were quiet for a while.

Mallory leaned forward and rubbed her hands together. "What you said, about being tired of keeping it a secret—I know what you mean. When I was in college, I had this thing with a professor—an affair, I guess. She was much older. She was an author who'd won awards for her work. She was totally brilliant; she'd say these things offhandedly, as if they were afterthoughts, that changed how I saw everything. She was also the first woman I'd ever been with."

"And you never told anyone about it?"

"Well," Mallory said, "she was married to a man at the time. And she was very successful. I didn't want to ruin her life. I just wanted to be a part of it."

"Imagine if that all came out now. She'd be screwed."

"What do you mean?"

"She was your professor."

"She was *a* professor," said Mallory. "She wasn't *mine*."

"Still," said Caroline. "She was a professor at the school where you were a student."

Mallory picked up the steel poker beside her and stoked the fire. "It's nothing like what people are talking about."

She didn't like this version of her relationship with the woman, though it was possible their affair would be frowned upon even more so now. *Was this what the woman had meant*, wondered Mallory, *that their time together would no longer be only hers?*

"Sorry," Caroline said now. "I thought that's what you meant about ruining her life."

"Maybe," said Mallory. "Although, at first, I kind of loved not telling anyone. It was like this story in a book I had tucked away somewhere that only I could find. But then I started looking for little openings whenever I was talking to another person. You know when you have something you want to tell someone else and you try to naturally steer the conversation in a direction that will make it easier to reveal that thing? But even when the moment seemed right, I couldn't do it."

"Why not?"

"I don't know. Why haven't you told anyone about the finance guy?"

"In a weird way, I guess I thought it didn't matter. The me that was in that relationship was not the me next to you right now. Even though it was only a few years ago, it was like a whole other life lived by a whole other person. Is that how you feel?"

"Pretty much the opposite. I think the me that's next to you right now is only here because of my relationship with her."

Caroline reached out her hand and held Mallory's. "I'm not sure if I'm grateful to her or upset with her."

It would always be that way, Mallory suspected.

She looked down at her hand braided with Caroline's and saw that Caroline's knuckles were cracked with eczema. Almost without thinking, Mallory brought the rough skin to her lips. Caroline laughed, soft and sweet. Their eyes met, and they each gave a smile like a wince, as if it hurt to be happy.

Mallory nudged the fire a final time. She prodded the soft parts of the wood, causing embers to shoot up before fading. She unzipped her sweatshirt a little to feel some of the warmth on her chest.

They went to bed that night underneath the stars, gazing up through the glass roof of the house at the clear and sparkling sky. When Mallory woke the next morning, Caroline was making coffee. Daybreak had been dimmed by a window scrim, and when Mallory pulled it open, staggering, unflinching sunshine suddenly flooded the tiny house. It was a lot of light. Everywhere she looked, even if she closed her eyes, there it was. She felt there was nothing between her and the overwhelming brightness of the world.

ACKNOWLEDGMENTS

Thank you, first and foremost, to my dad, my best friend, without whom this literally would not be possible.

To Sarah Burnes, for seeing something in me and in this book from the start and for her support that never wavered. Sarah, this is a "real book" because of you.

To Laura Perciasepe, for the wonderful conversation years ago at Momofuku and for all the wonderful conversations—including the ones in Track Changes—since. Even before we met, I think this book was meant for you.

To Halimah Marcus and Brandon Taylor from Electric Literature, who plucked my weird short story from the slush pile and gave it a home. You guys changed my life.

To Akhil Sharma, the most brilliant writer, whom I've been really fortunate to have as a mentor.

To Lydia Hirt, whom I was lucky enough to sit next to at my very first publishing lunch. To everyone at Riverhead, who's made publishing a debut feel like a homecoming.

To Patrick Ryan, the best first editor a girl could ask for.

To Tayari Jones, whose lessons—both about art and life—are forever reverberating. To Martha McPhee for the early encouragement, for telling me that writing was a possibility. To Alice Elliott Dark, Jayne Anne Philips, Lee Zimmerman, William Hutnik, Tara Malia, and Nancy Norbeck.

To Anabel Graff, a great friend and a great writer, who helped and humored me for years while I tried to figure this thing out. Ditto Nick Masercola and Sarah Niebuhr. Thanks also to Brian Skulnik, Iris Harris, Megan Cummins, Laura Spence-Ash, Laura Villareal, and John Bryans for the very early reads.

To the team at *O*: Leigh Haber, Lisa Kogan, Elena Nicolau, Naomi Barr, Lisa DeLisle, Adrienne Girard, Arianna Davis, Joseph Zambrano, Gayle King, and of course, Oprah.

And to Candice Singh, my partner in time, my reason for getting up in the morning.